Night Mare

Written and Illustrated
By
Maria Dahlen
&
Sage Stanley

AuthorHouse™ LLC
1663 Liberty Drive
Bloomington, IN 47403
www.authorhouse.com
Phone: 1-800-839-8640

© 2014 Maria Dahlen and Sage Stanley. All rights reserved.

No part of this book may be reproduced, stored in a retrieval system, or transmitted by any means without the written permission of the author.

Published by AuthorHouse 02/19/2014

ISBN: 978-1-4918-6397-8 (sc)
ISBN: 978-1-4918-6396-1 (e)

Library of Congress Control Number: 2014902668

Any people depicted in stock imagery provided by Thinkstock are models, and such images are being used for illustrative purposes only.
Certain stock imagery © Thinkstock.

This book is printed on acid-free paper.

Because of the dynamic nature of the Internet, any web addresses or links contained in this book may have changed since publication and may no longer be valid. The views expressed in this work are solely those of the author and do not necessarily reflect the views of the publisher, and the publisher hereby disclaims any responsibility for them.

Dedicated to:

It all began
with the usual
'Once Upon
A Time....'

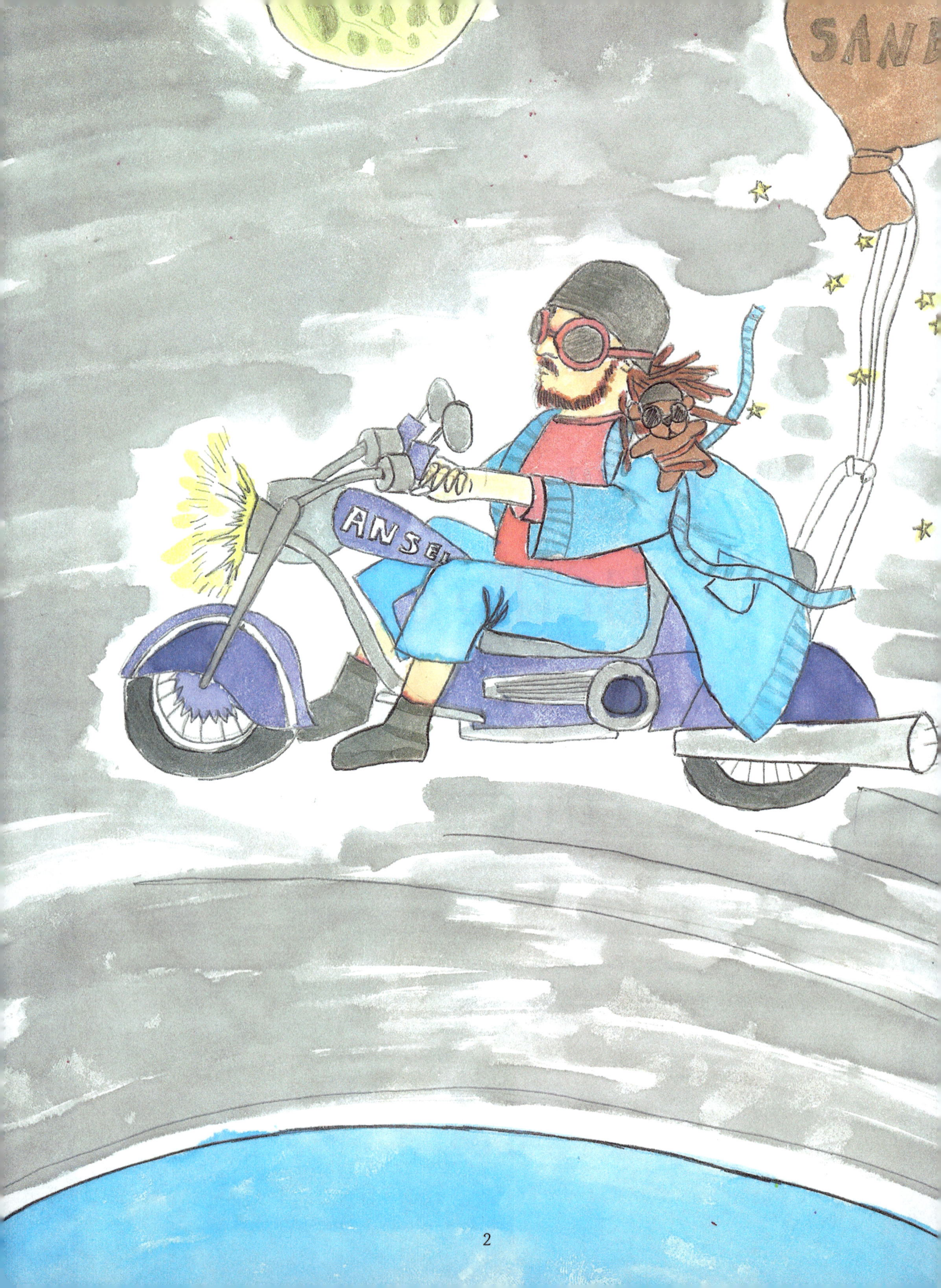
SANB
ANSE

Sandman scurried across the world nightly to give Earth's population the precious gift of sleep. Since the population increased daily however, he was finding it more and more difficult to keep up with the demand. Though immortal, he too wasn't getting any younger, and he was growing increasingly desperate for help.

4

Sandman sat slumped at his desk. He was exhausted after another long night of spreading his golden sleeping sands about the Earth. Though tired, he knew that doing nothing about his situation wouldn't help improve things. The problem would only keep getting worse by the night. So, taking quill to parchment, Sandman set about writing an ad for help.

Wanted:

An energetic intern.
Long hours but lots of prestige.
Apply in person **ASAP**.

Sandman

Looking over the finished ad, Sandman couldn't imagine who would take such a position . . . . The hours certainly weren't good. This person would need to be time-oriented, dependable, courageous, and people-friendly. Having no other options, Sandman sent out the advertisement anyway . . . hoping.

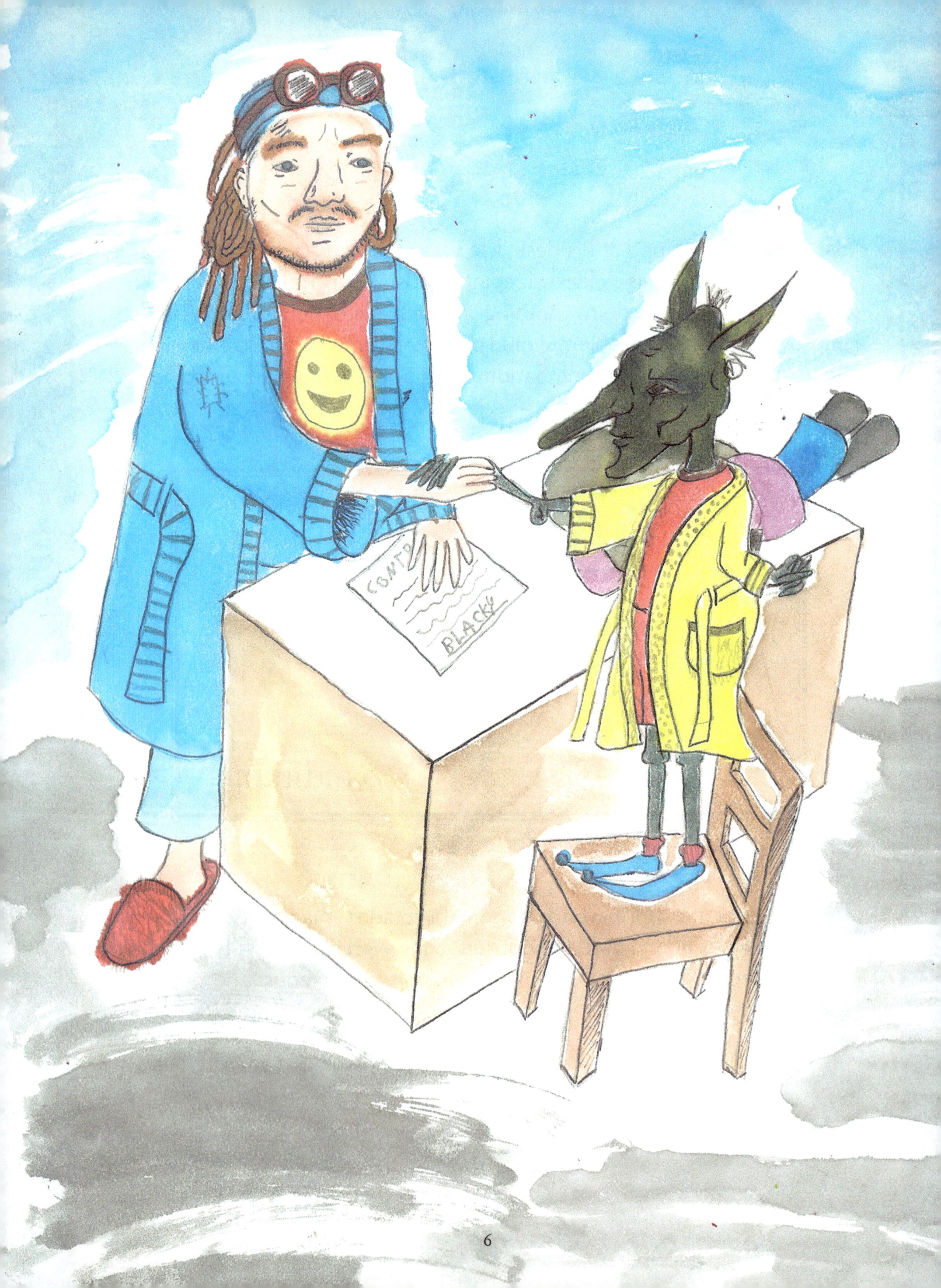
BLACKY

As expected, there was very little interest in the position within the magical realm in which Sandman lived. In fact, the only person who showed up for an interview was a mean looking little troll named Blackie. Sandman looked upon the beady-eyed little figure and sighed. Though not 100% confident in his decision . . . resume unseen, credentials unchecked, Blackie was hired. Sandman was desperate.

Blackie, in fact, was a bad choice for the internship position. He was lazy; he took short cuts; he was never on time; he skipped many of the households on his assigned route. In fact he just plain hated people in general as he found them to be rather dull. He had only taken the job as the Sandman's intern because he was bored, out of work, penniless, and needed to find a new "racket" for himself. Blackie figured Sandman's job would fix his first three problems, and at least give him some good leads on how to fix the fourth.

SAND

One of the few households that Blackie did manage to visit on his nightly route was that of the Mare family. This fluke had more to do with the Mare's place on his work route than anything else.

The Mares were a mother and daughter household. They lived in a somewhat old, rundown little house at the edge of Rocky Forest. What the house lacked in repair and modernity however, it more than made up for with its' comforts and charm. Each room was filled with brick-a-brac, worn, over-stuffed chairs, and love.

One night Blackie found the Mare house just too inviting to simply blow some sand around in the dark and pass on. The comfy chair by the crackling fire looked so very, very tempting. And, he was so tired—tired of coming up with excuses and finding ways of not working.

Room to room Blackie went with a scant pinch of his golden sleeping sands and carelessly blew them into the darkness, assuming that the sands would reach the intended targets and put the household to sleep. The little troll then hurried over to settle himself in the over-stuffed chair by the fire. He placed his ginormous bag of golden sleeping sand under his feet as a foot rest and immediately fell asleep.

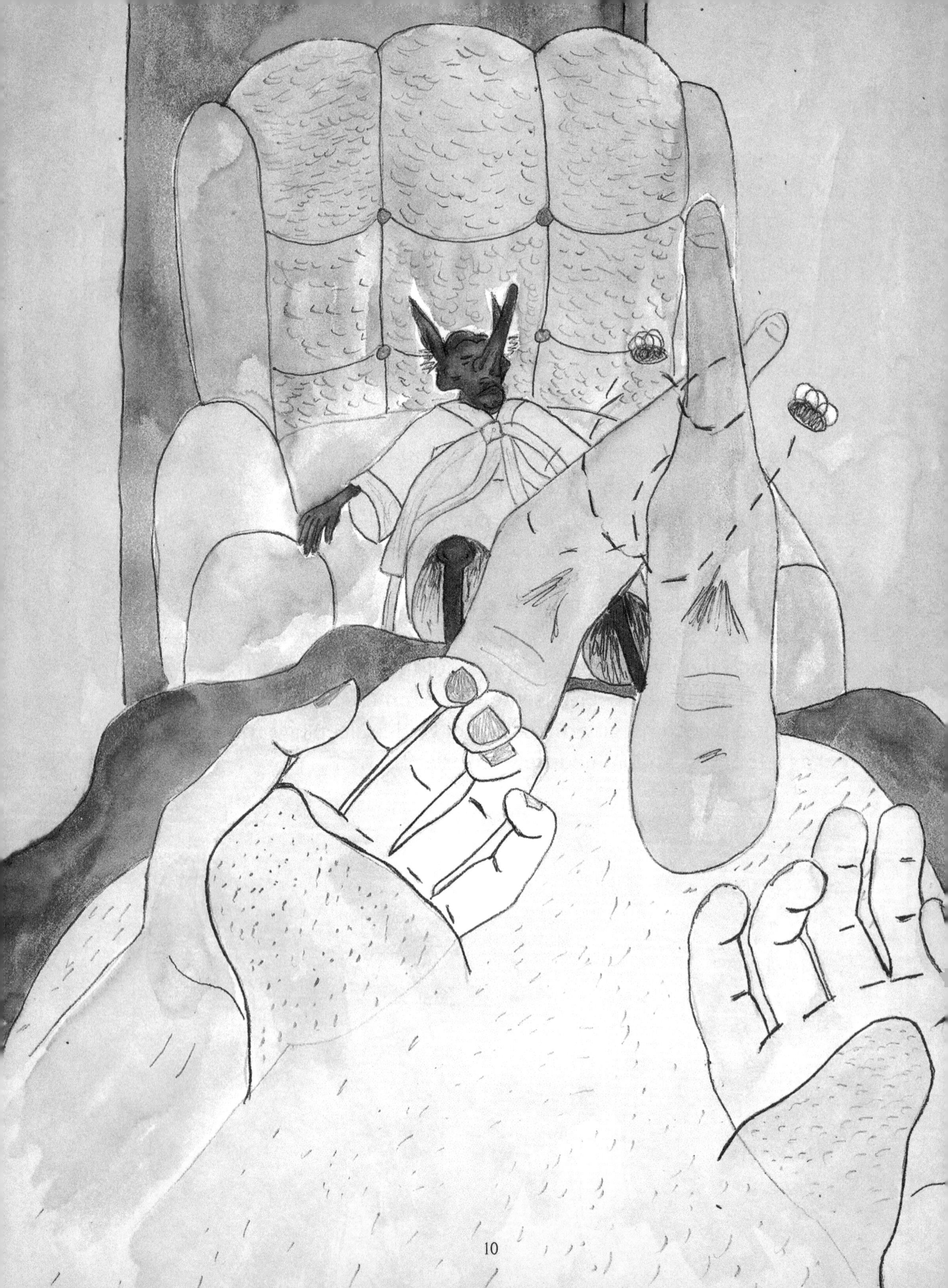

Back in her bedroom, Sage indeed had not been hit by the sleeping sands. Hearing strange noises coming from the other room, much like an excited toad burping, she decided to investigate. Peeking out into the darkened hallway toward the living room, Sage saw the room sparkle and glow golden, as the sands reflected the firelight and bounced playfully upon the walls.

Sage gasped out loud. "How beautiful!" she whispered.

Creeping forward toward the living room, Sage saw a little troll sleeping in the overstuffed chair by the fire. He was a tiny, blackish-green, wrinkled form with a long nose and pointed ears. The tufts of white hair growing out of his ears were caked in dried ear wax and dandruff. 'How odd!' she thought to herself. Sage then spotted the ginormous bag of golden sand that lay beneath the troll's pointy-shoed feet. Suddenly she understood who he was and why he and his sand were there.

A wonderfully mischievous idea sprang into Sage's head. Quickly she sat down on the floor next to the troll and his sack and filled one of her socks with the magical sand. Once she was sure she had enough, she snuck back to her bedroom unnoticed.

Blackie was long gone by morning.

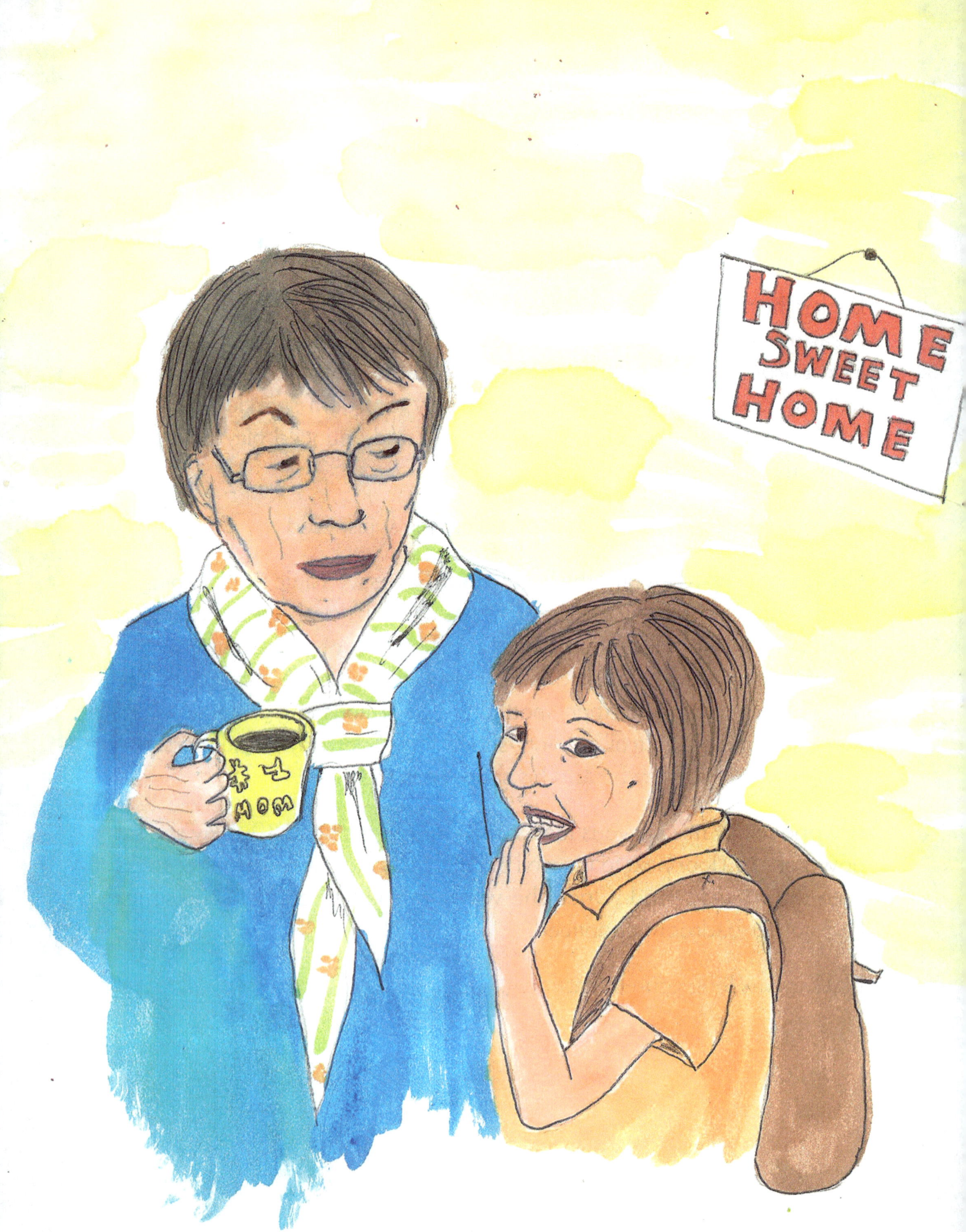
HOME
SWEET
HOME
MOM

The next morning, after a quick breakfast of porridge and juice, Sage and Mother Mare left the house to go their separate ways for the day. Mother Mare had more resumes to distribute about the village. She had lost her job recently and was actively looking for work. Sage, on the other hand, was unusually eager to get to school. Her mother was suspicious of this new-found urgency for school, but shrugged it off to the fickleness of youth.

Patting her bulging sock in anticipation, Sage kissed her mother's cheek and hurried off.

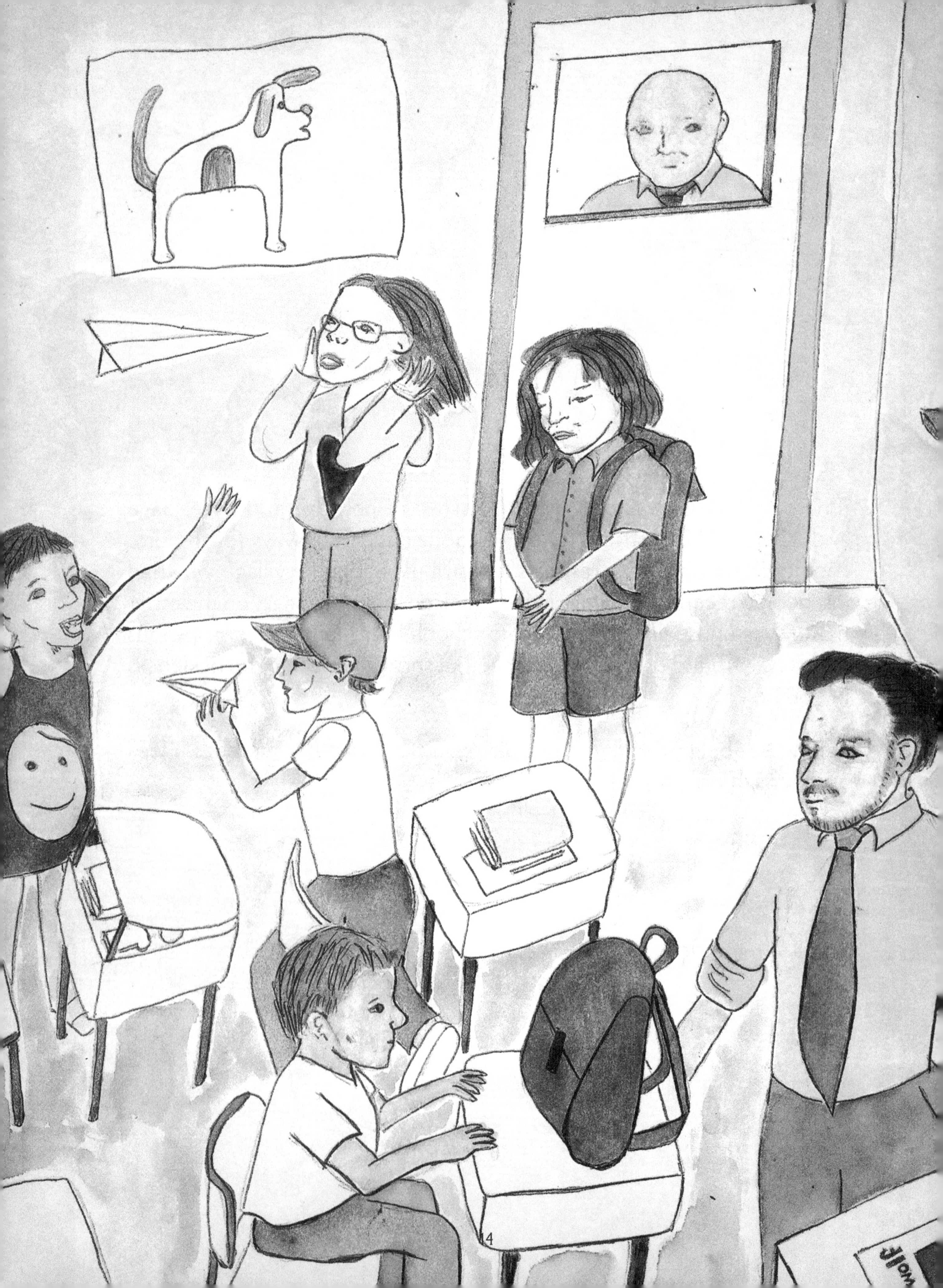

The little Mare girl smiled at Micah as she entered her classroom and made her way to her desk. Sage thought that he was cute, with his dark curly hair and dimpled chin. Micah however had yet to acknowledge her. "That will soon change!" she mumbled to herself, smiling.

16

As his class settled in at their desks ready to begin a new school day, Mr. B, the math teacher, cleared his throat. He had a surprise for them. "Pop quiz!" he called, chuckling as his students let out a collective groan.

No one groaned louder than Sage though. She had been so busy sketching hearts declaring 'Sage plus Micah' that she hadn't cracked her math book in over a week. She was more than sure she would fail the quiz. A smile came to her lips then and quickly spread across her face. 'This would be the perfect opportunity to test the golden sleeping sands!' she told herself.

Mr. B was now walking up and down the aisles between the students' desks, handing out a really difficult looking quiz that had all sorts of funny and unrecognizable formulas printed upon it. "Class, please put everything away in your desks except a pencil."

When Mr. B reached Sage's desk, she leaned over, pretending to have an itch, and reached for her sock. With a small amount of the golden sleeping sand firmly in hand, she straightened and blew a golden cloud right at Mr. B.

Mr. B didn't know what hit him. He and three students who were also in the path of the sand were immediately put to sleep where they sat, or stood.

18

The pop quiz was cancelled. Principal Carlson called for an early recess. All of the school windows and doors were opened to air out the school and wake the sleepy-heads.

"**Recess!**" kids screamed. Not needing to be told twice, the entire student population quickly emptied the building and made a mad rush for the playground.

Sage sat on one of the swings. She gawked at Micah who was on the monkey bars with a bunch of other boys from their class as they goofed off. Off to the side, by himself, Tyler sat. He was also watching. Tyler had a medical problem called muscular dystrophy which made him unable to use his muscles or communicate with words. Sage barely glanced at him. He was always 'watching.' Sometimes he really bothered her.

A small band of bullies suddenly appeared from the corner of the school. They were led by Peter, a tall white haired boy with cold blue eyes. Acting like they owned the playground, they raced up to Micah and his friends and began to hassle the boys.

Sage tensed. She hated that boy. She hated the whole bunch of them!

The bullies threw playground sand at Micah and his friends, and chased after them, calling them sissy names. Sand landed on Tyler also, but no one noticed.

Sage was furious. 'No one could push her boyfriend around!' She got up from her swing and marched over to the monkey bars and began chasing the bullies around the playground equipment, throwing a big fist-full of sand at the bullies to stop them.

Within minutes both Sage and the bullies were caught by the playground monitor and immediately ushered into the office.

"They started it!" Sage protested. She was still in trouble though.

There would be no more recess for any of them for the remainder of the week.

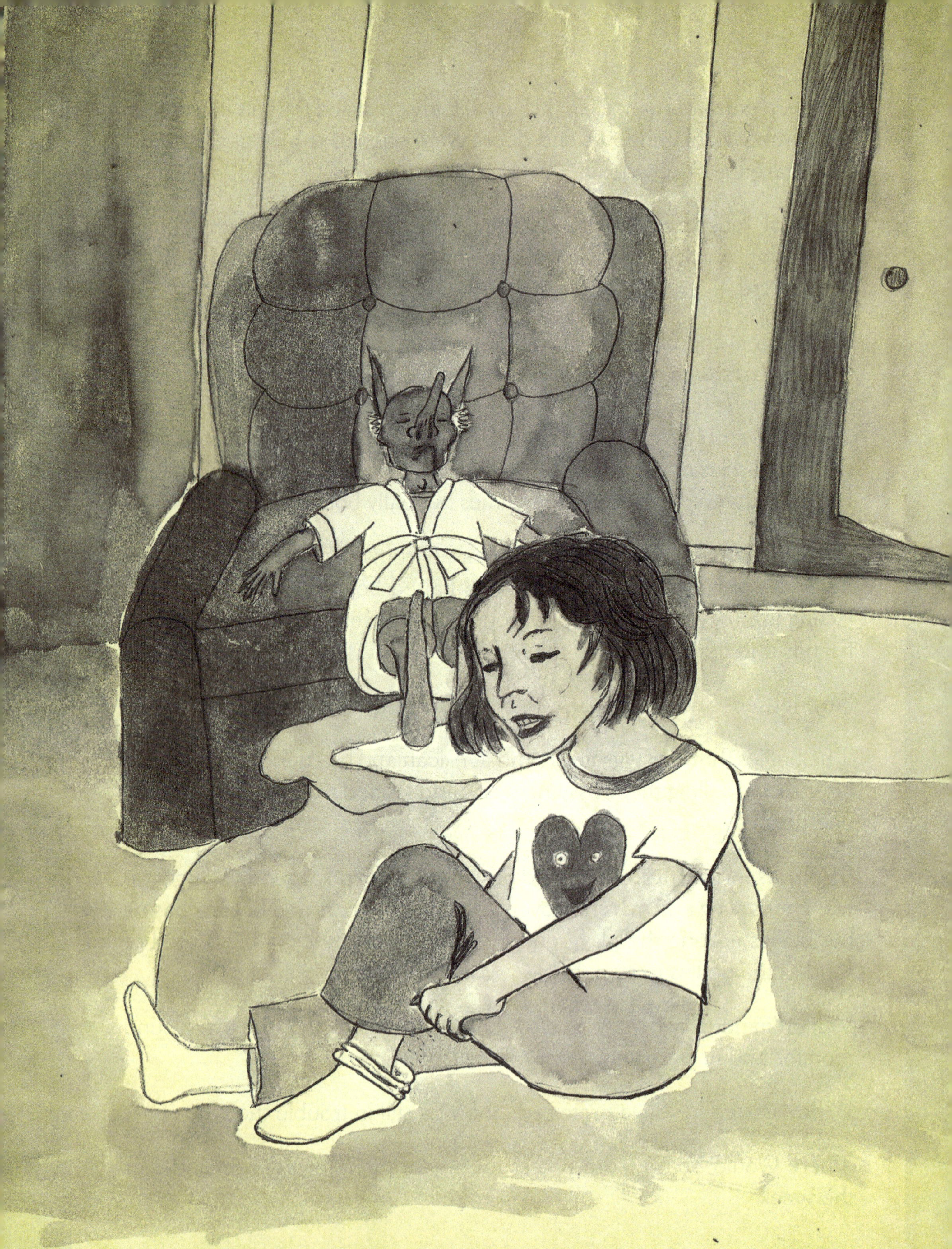

That night, exhausted from doing nothing interesting or good, and remembering the soft overstuffed chair and the welcoming fire at the Mare's house, Blackie returned. Following the same routine as the previous night, he halfheartedly blew a speck of the golden sleeping sand into each of the bedrooms from the doorways. Again the sand completely missed Sage. And, once again, she snuck out into the living room when the troll was asleep and helped herself to another sock full of golden sleeping sand.

There was a school assembly scheduled for the next morning, but Sage had a different plan in mind.

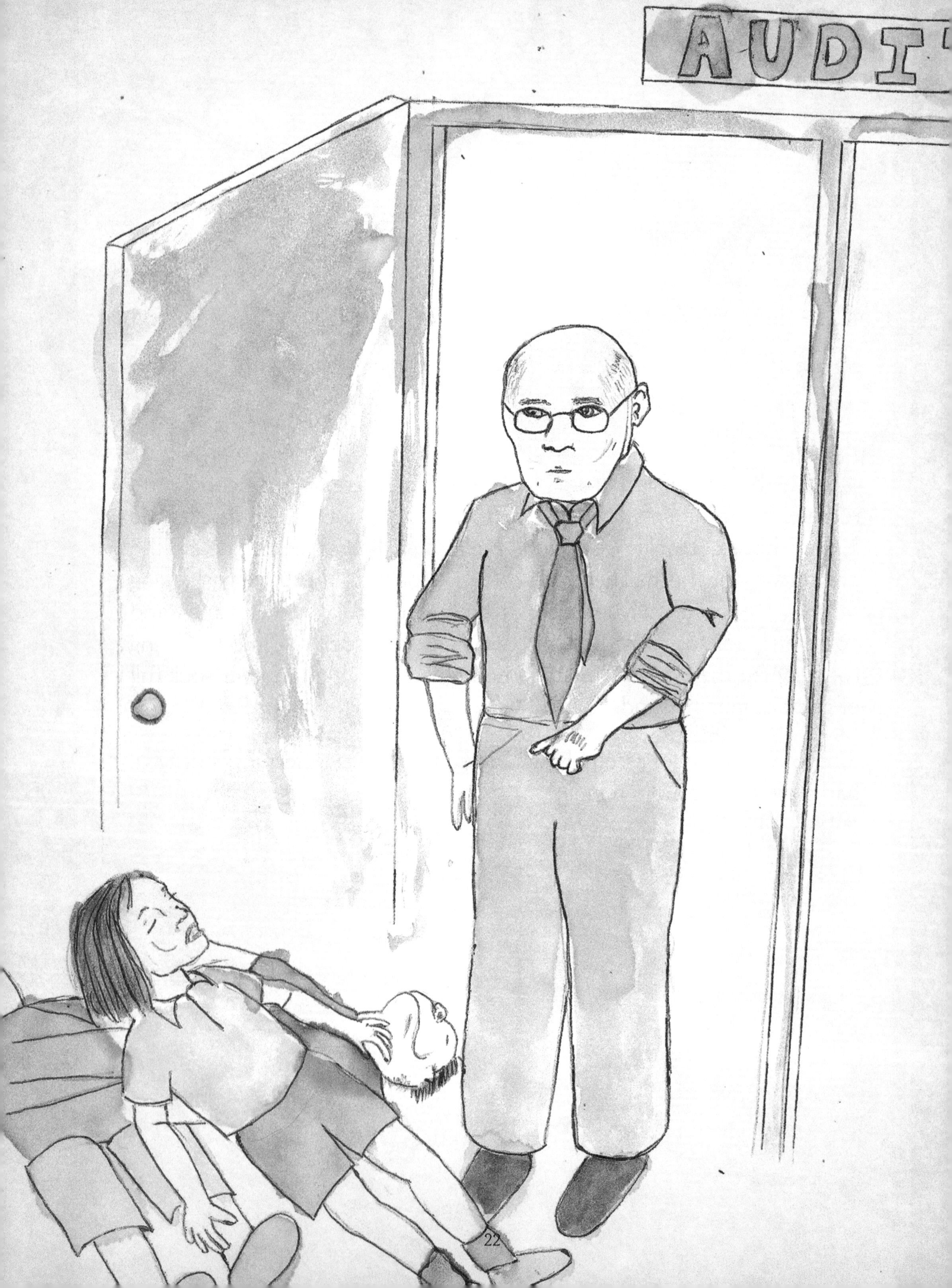
AUDI

Principal Carlson greeted the students the next day at the door to the auditorium before the program. The school was going to be treated to a lecture on stargazing in the night sky. The principal, however, didn't see that same small band of bullies from the previous day close behind in line as they shoved to try and make their way into the auditorium.

'This might be my best opportunity!' Sage thought to herself. She stealthily went for her sock by faking another itch. Just as she rose and was about to blow her handful of golden sleeping sand at the bullies however, the line was suddenly knocked forward several paces by these same boys. Her handful of sand was swept ahead into her own face and the faces of the other kids in line before her. Within seconds large sections of the line fell, imploding onto itself like Legos in one big heap before the Principal.

This time Principal Carlson had no question as to how his school was being put to sleep. 'It was Sage!' Sage's punishment would be much much worse than missing a week of recess, or a note sent home from school. This time, as soon as Sage woke up from her nap, she would be suspended from school for a week and would be in much more trouble at home.

ECTRIC
OGALOO

Mother Mare was in the middle of a job interview when she received an urgent phone call from school. She was told to pick up her slumbering daughter since she had been suspended. Her family desperately needed her to get this job at the Pixie Sweets Manufacturing Plant. Mother Mare had been unemployed for nearly a year and things were desperate at home.

Not only did Mother Mare take a personal call during the interview, which is considered a 'no, no!', but in all of the commotion she accidently dumped the interviewer's coffee across a desk full of papers. The papers had been ruined, and the interviewer hastily waved Mrs. Mare out of the plant.

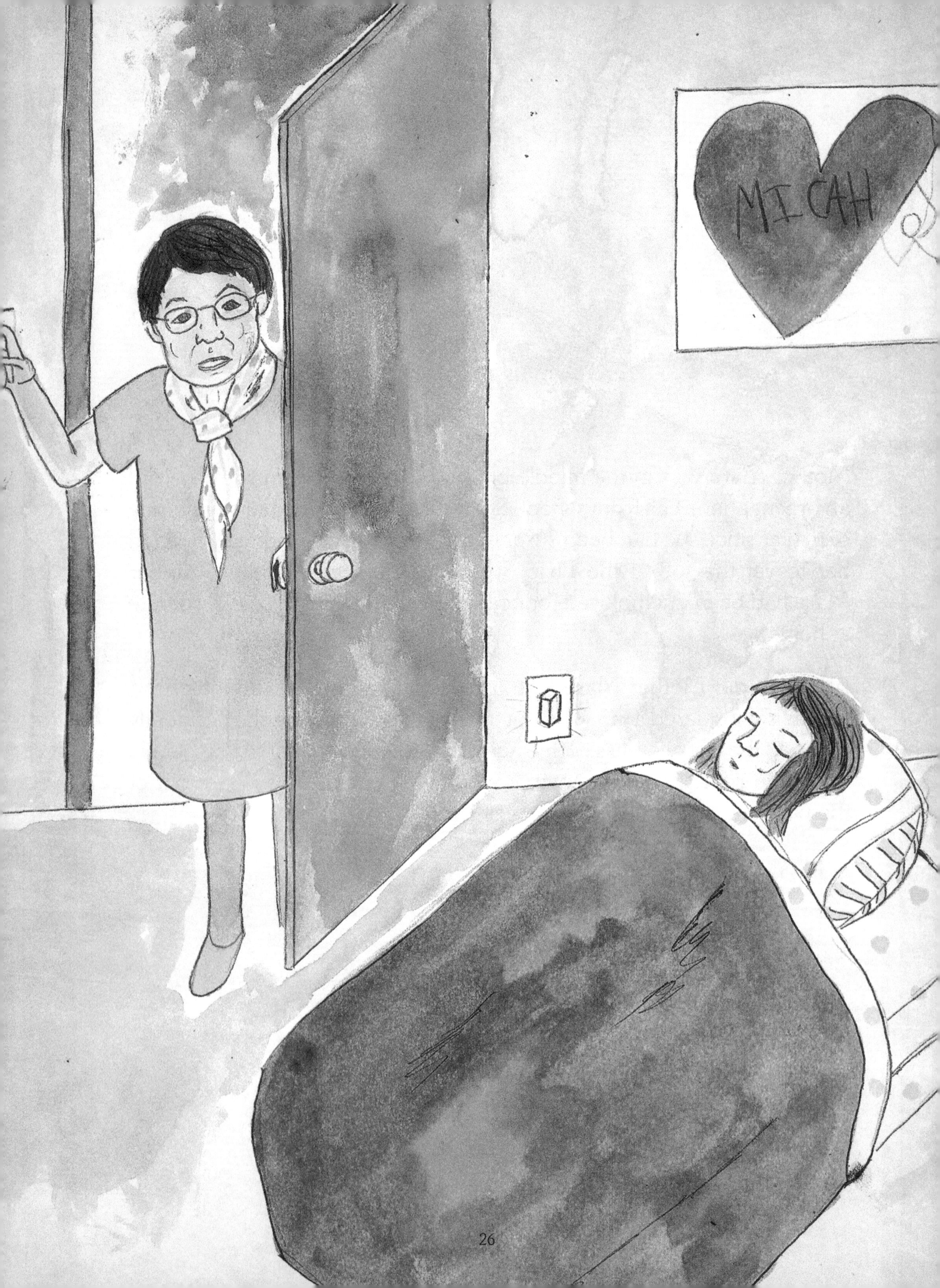
MICAH

"How could you do such a thing?" Mother Mare screeched as she made her way home with her sleeping daughter. She wasn't sure that her daughter was really still asleep and not able to hear her. Mother Mare suspected that Sage was now faking being asleep to avoid confrontation. "I am so disappointed in you! You can just stay in your room for the rest of the evening!" Without another word Mother Mare tucked her daughter into bed and left the room, slamming the door angrily behind her.

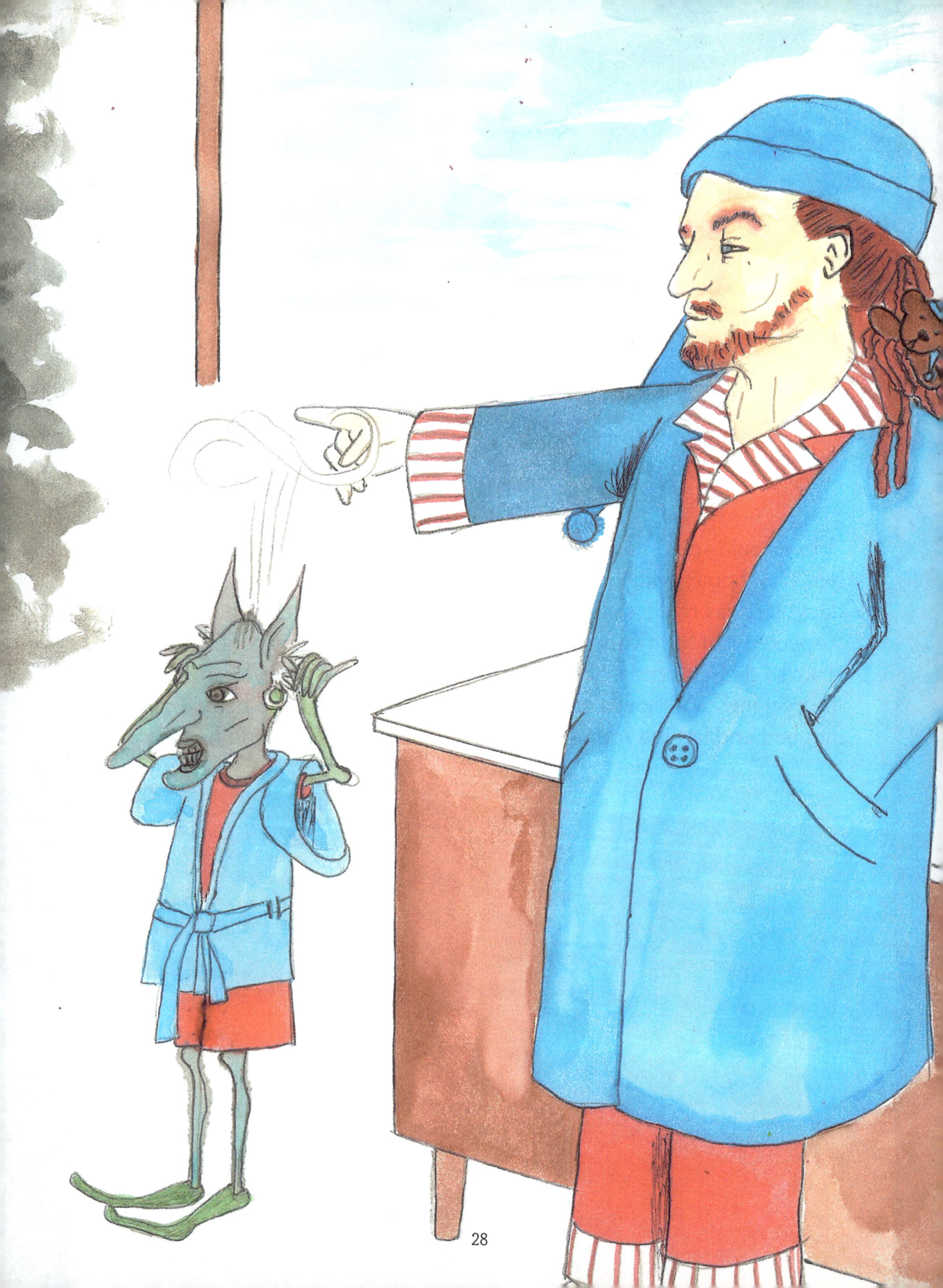

Sandman's intern Blackie was also in trouble. The Sandman had received thousands of complaints about Blackie from every part of the world. He now called the little troll on his slacking off and the steadily depleting inventory of golden sleeping sand. Despite the troll's pleadings and promises to do better, there was nothing Blackie could do or say to change Sandman's mind. He was fired!

In his mind though, Blackie believed that none of the complaints against him were his fault. All he wanted to know now was who had been stealing his golden sleeping sand. He was determined that he would find out and make sure that person paid for getting him fired!

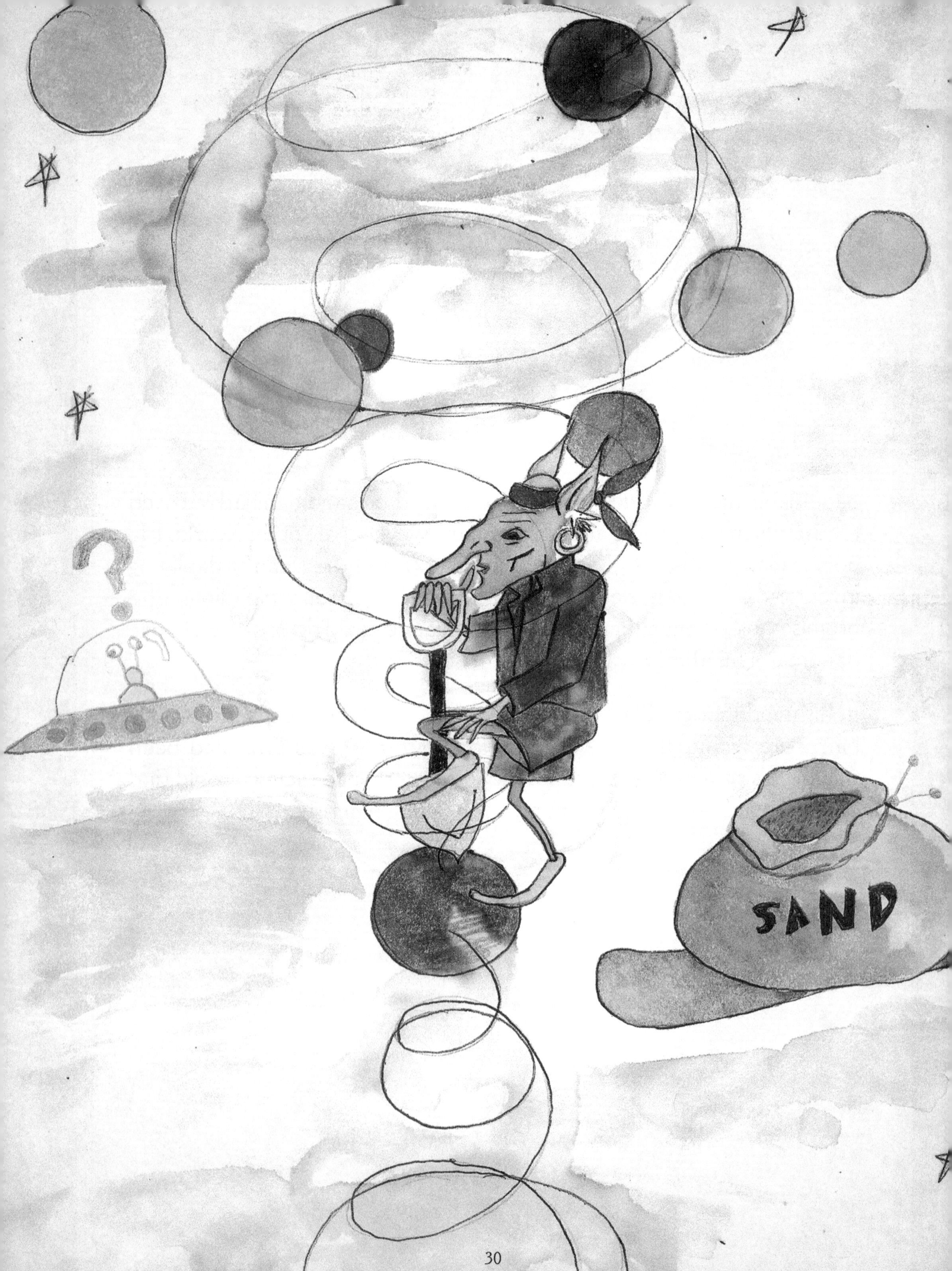
SAND

Blackie still had a bit of golden sleeping sand leftover, stashed in his possession. Having plenty of time on his hands now, that night Blackie put himself to sleep. It was a long, hard sleep where he dreamed that he was sucked deep down into the inner core of a black hole. There, his dream-self harvested the black hole's dark and weighty anti-matter that stretched miserably before him. These were the nightmare sands of the mortal realm. Then, as quickly and magically as he had gotten there, the dream ended. Blackie woke up in his own hovel with a ginormous bag of sparkling black sand that he had just harvested next to his bed.

Armed for revenge, Blackie set off to re-trace his steps and find the one who had stolen the golden sleeping sands from him and had gotten him fired.

ON THE WAY OF THE HALE KINGS
ODE TO THE PEANUT BUTTE SANDWICH
L O V E
NIGHT MARE
BLACKIE
SAND

Not quite halfway through his never before completed route, Blackie came upon the Mare's house. Again, he settled into the home's comforts. A nagging thought now dogged him. 'Could the people who lived here have stolen his sands? He had certainly spent enough time there to have presented an opportunity for someone there to do so.' The troll decided that he would find out.

Following the same routine as the previous nights, Blackie halfheartedly blew the last couple grains of his golden sleeping sand into the two bedrooms. As always, the sand completely missed Sage. Then Blackie settled himself into the soft, snuggly, oversized chair, and waited. He peeked out at the room through slit eyes, hoping beyond hope that someone would come and prove him right before he accidently fell asleep.

As before, once she was pretty sure that the troll had fallen asleep, Sage snuck out into the living room. She planned to take another sock-full of golden sleeping sand. This time however, the sand was not to be used as a plaything for pranks. This time her plan was to make everything right and fix things both at school and with her mother's job interview.

Sure that the troll was again asleep, Sage plopped herself down on the floor next to him. Eagerly she dug both her hands deeply into the ginormous bag, not noticing that the sands did not glow gold. These sands were instead a sparkling jet black, more course and quartz-like than the sleeping sands had been. Sage did notice however that she couldn't lift any of the sand, not even one grain from the bag. Its gravitational weight was too great for her to manage. Her hands were now stuck in the sand.

Now, opening his eyes wide, with one fell swoop, Blackie sprang up from the overstuffed chair. He leaned forward, grabbed one of Sage's wrists from the bag, and held her tightly in his long, crooked, pickle-like fingers.

34

Blackie stared at the little girl with an evil and unwavering eye. He cackled vengefully through withered black lips, "For making me lose my job little girl . . . I condemn both you and Sandman! You—you will become Night Mare. You will become a black horse, forever galloping through the night as you follow Sandman on his route around the Earth. I will be your rider. Together we shall spread these black sands across the Earth, dispensing bad dreams in Sandman's wake. Sandman will forever be condemned to not catching up to us to stop the cycle of mayhem that we shall cause. Sandman will be ruined! Ruined I say! Heh heh heh heh!" he chuckled.

With that, the little troll reached into the bag of sparkling black sand. The weight was nothing to a creature of the magical realm. Then he blew a handful of the magic sand into the terrified little girl's face. Before disappearing, the troll left her with the ominous words . . ."I'll be back!"

Immediately Sage fell into a deep and troubled sleep. Her mind clouded with dark and terrible images. Her body ached as it began morphing into unknown dimensions and became infected by the nightmarish black sands.

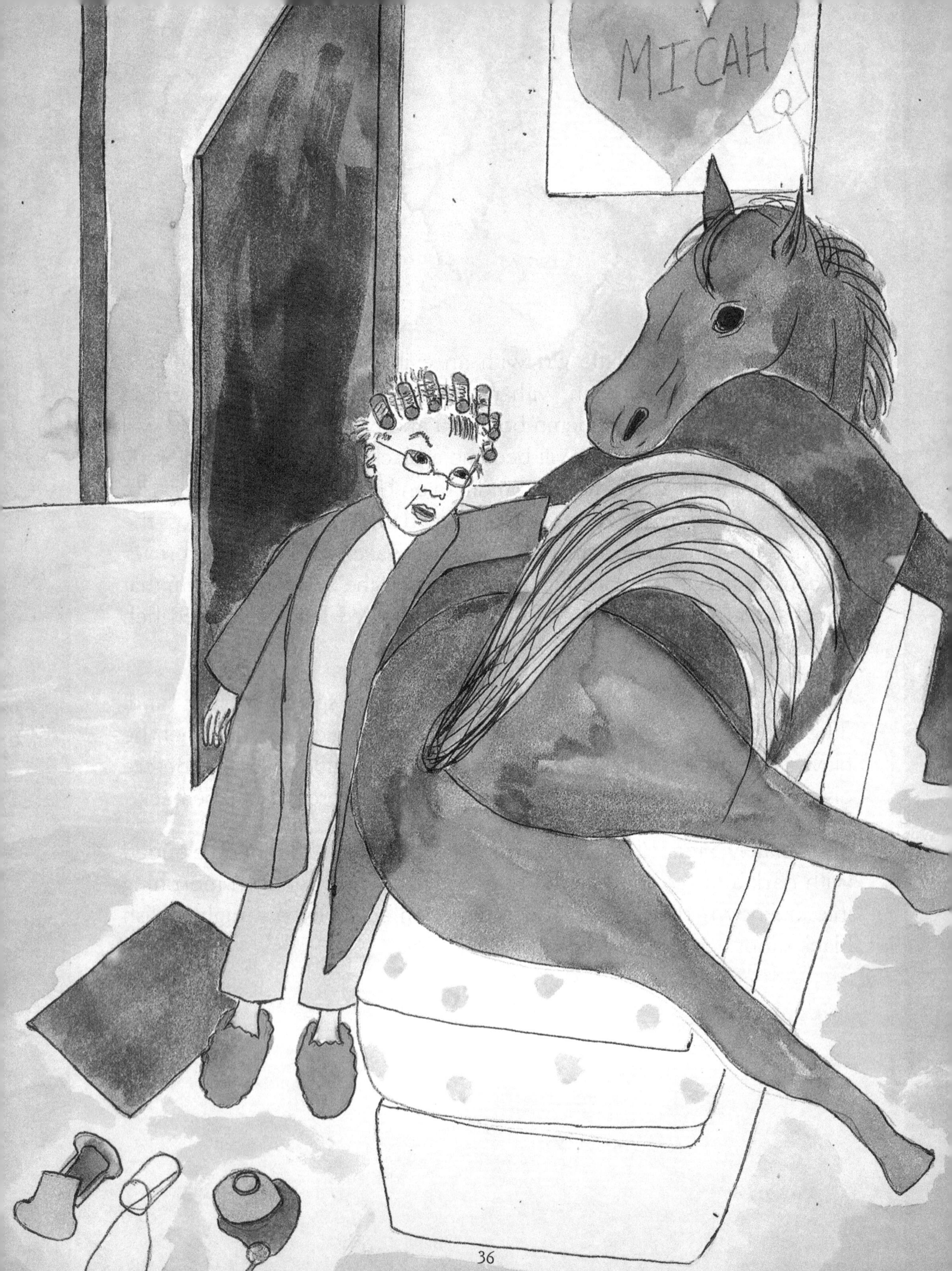
MICAH

Having calmed down a bit, Mother Mare crept into Sage's room with a tray of dinner later that evening. She was sure that Sage would be awake by now. She wanted to tell her daughter that she still loved her, despite her earlier rage. Now, not quite so angry, she wanted to discuss what had happened and to ask her daughter why she had done what she had. Inside Sage's bedroom, Mother Mare found her daughter tossing and turning in her sleep, burning with fever. Her small form now seemed too big for the bed as it pulsated and seemed to grow ever bigger as it tossed.

The dinner tray fell to the floor with a loud crash. Mother Mare just knew that something was terribly terribly wrong. She sat down on the edge of Sage's bed and wrapped her arms around her daughter to comfort her, and kiss her, and try to figure out what was wrong so that she could help.

Immediately upon being kissed, Sage finished morphing into her new form and rolled out of bed. The covers fell from her limbs to reveal the once small and pretty girl to now be a large midnight black horse with enormous rippling muscles and fiery red eyes.

Mother Mare jumped back, aghast. She wanted to scream, but stood silent from shock.

But the love that had emanated from her mother's kiss broke part of Blackie's spell. Sage was no longer compelled to gallop through the night bringing mayhem and fright to sleepers. Blackie would not be riding her. Scared and confused though, and not wanting to accidentally hurt her mother with her enormous new form, Sage, or rather Night Mare, bolted from the house, still consigned to follow Sandman on his nightly route.

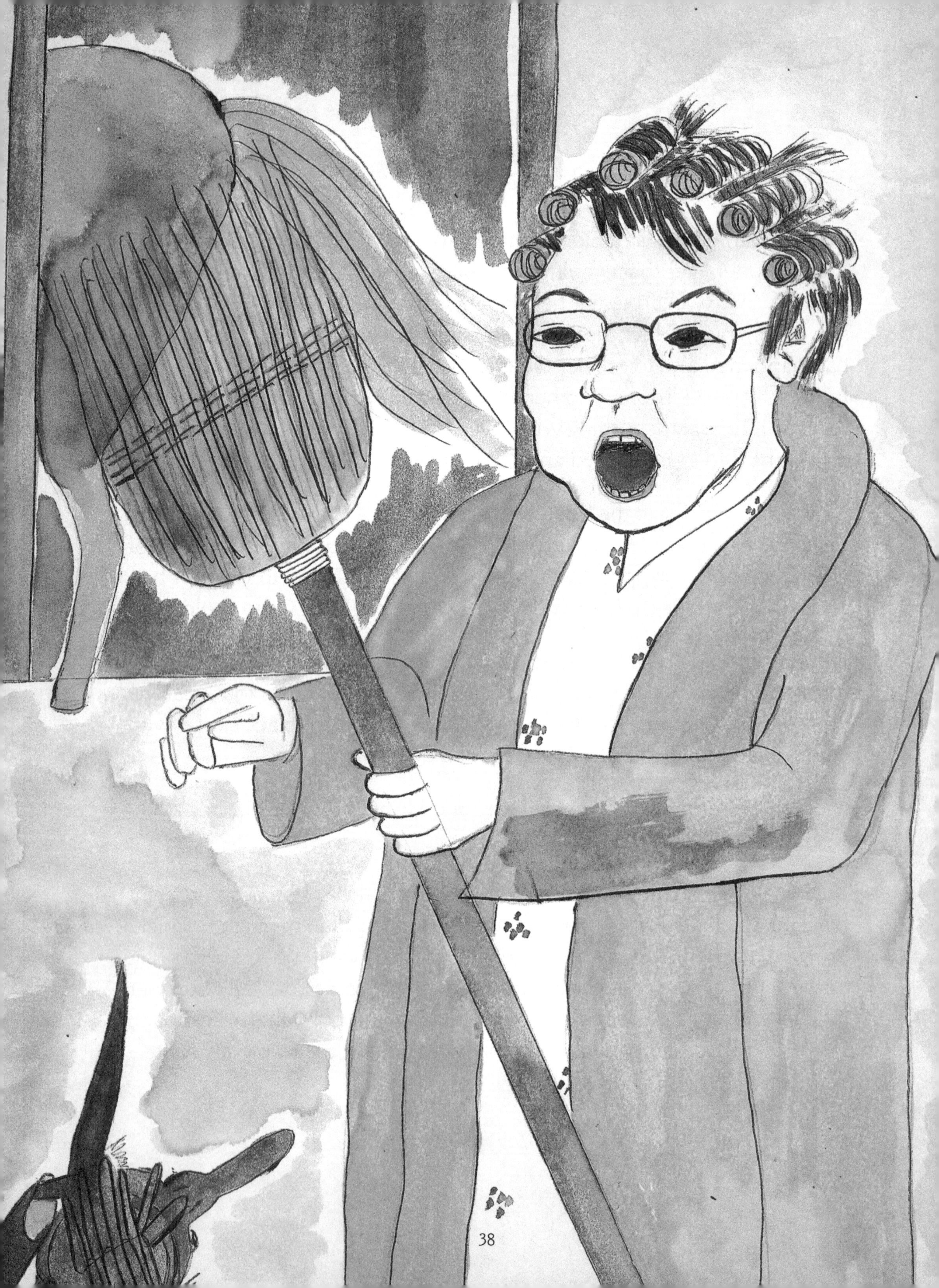

Acting instinctively now, Mother Mare tried to grab her daughter, to hold the black mare from going, but couldn't. "I love you and will fight for you!" she called out after her daughter with a sob as her daughter galloped away.

Suddenly, in a puff of smoke, Blackie appeared. Without uttering a word, seeing Night Mare race off, the troll quickly vanished from the house to follow her. Mother Mare's broom swatted at him as he disappeared.

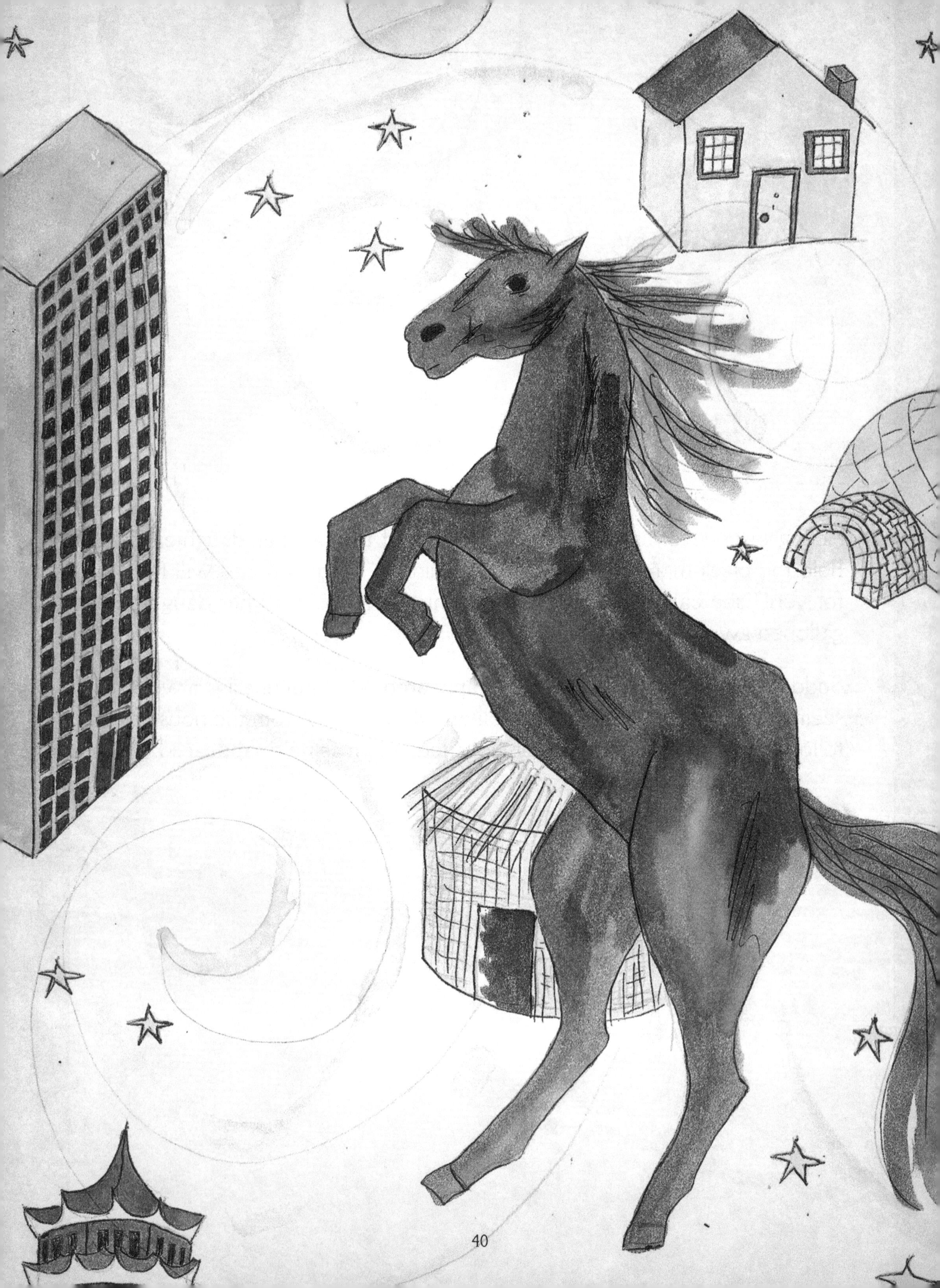

Through the night Sage, as Night Mare, galloped with blazing speed, following Sandman's route. She hoped that she could pick up her pace and eventually catch up with him, to convince him to change her back.

As Night Mare galloped on, she saw mansions and shanties, town homes, tree houses, dugouts, apartments, trailer homes, log cabins, igloos, and everything in between. She noted that everyone's home was unique to its' inhabitants. She wished that everyone could see what she was seeing now – how truly unique everyone was on the inside and could respect and appreciate others differences.

But Night Mare knew that Blackie was following through with his plan to spread bad dreams, despite her not carrying him. As the occupants of these homes slept, their dreams were filled with terror as their dream-selves played out their nightmares. She had to push herself on – faster and faster through the night!

42

Sage's classmates were on her route. As Night Mare she grew to appreciate them more as she learned of their dreams and fears. She found out that Micah really did like her. He was afraid however of the bullying getting worse if he chose to 'notice' her. She saw Micah's dream-self playing out different scenarios of befriending her. All of his dreams ended up with him being teased by the bullies.

Sage, as Night Mare, also found out that the bullies were terrified of becoming victims of bullying themselves. She saw that this was why they acted out in the first place, trying to protect themselves. Peter and the others were afraid that no one would like them or want to be their friends. They thought bullying was the easiest way to deal with their fears. Saddest of all, bullying others had become so ingrained in these boys that they didn't know if they could act any other way even if they wanted to.

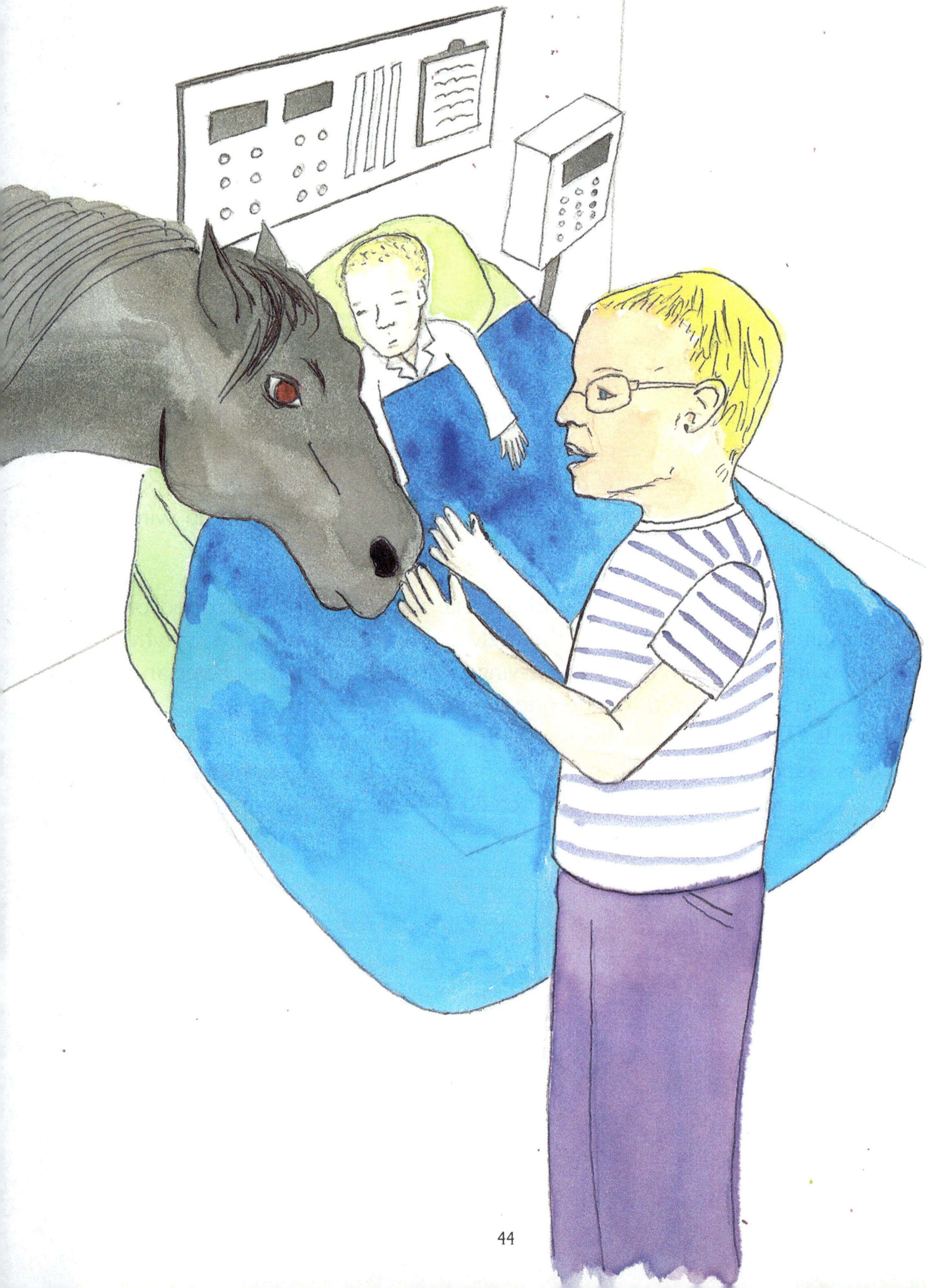

And then, Sage as Night Mare, came upon Tyler's house.

"Hello Sage!" Tyler called happily as Night Mare galloped into his bedroom.

Night Mare whinnied and reared in surprise. No one had seemed to see her before now, as they acted out their fears in their dreams.

"It's okay!" the small boy told her as he reached up to pet the towering, muscled mare's shiny black coat. "What's happened to you?" he asked.

Night Mare didn't recognize the boy. How did he know her? 'Who are you?' she tried to ask, but only a gruff snort managed to pass through her nostrils and lips. She looked over at the bed where the sleeping form of a small child lay in the dark. He was in a high-set hospital bed with lots of machinery surrounding him. It was Tyler. She now recognized him. The boy before her seemed so different from the Tyler she knew at school! 'How is this possible?' she wondered.

"Can I ride you?" Tyler asked. "How fast can you go? Have you always turned into a horse in your dreams? How did you get into my dream?" he continued.

Question after question flew from his once mute lips. Sage didn't know where to begin. She felt so overwhelmed by all of his questions that she couldn't begin to answer. Night Mare began backing up uneasily, prancing at the door to escape, but it wasn't time to leave. How come Tyler could see her when nobody else she visited could? Perhaps everyone else was too wrapped up in their nightmares to notice her?'

"It's okay. I'm not going to hurt you!" Tyler told her, putting a gentle hand on the rearing mare.

"How?" both asked simultaneously, and then each smiled, knowing then that sleep could be a great equalizer.

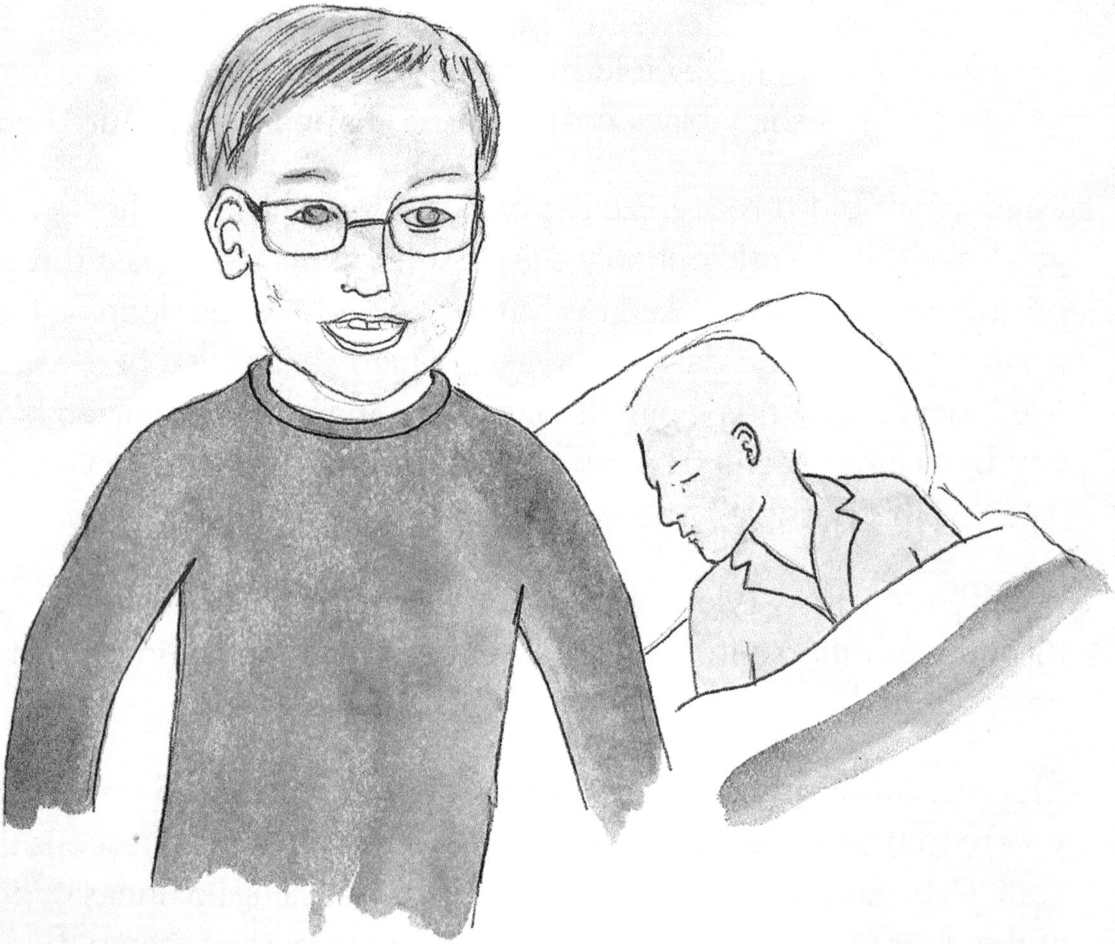

"How can you see me? Why aren't you afraid of me?" Night Mare blurted out with a flash of her fiery red eyes.

Tyler replied boldly then. "In my dreams I'm not afraid of anything. I can do anything! I don't have nightmares." His expression changed and he became sad then. "It's when I wake up – that I'm 'invisible.'" He stopped there.

And Sage understood.

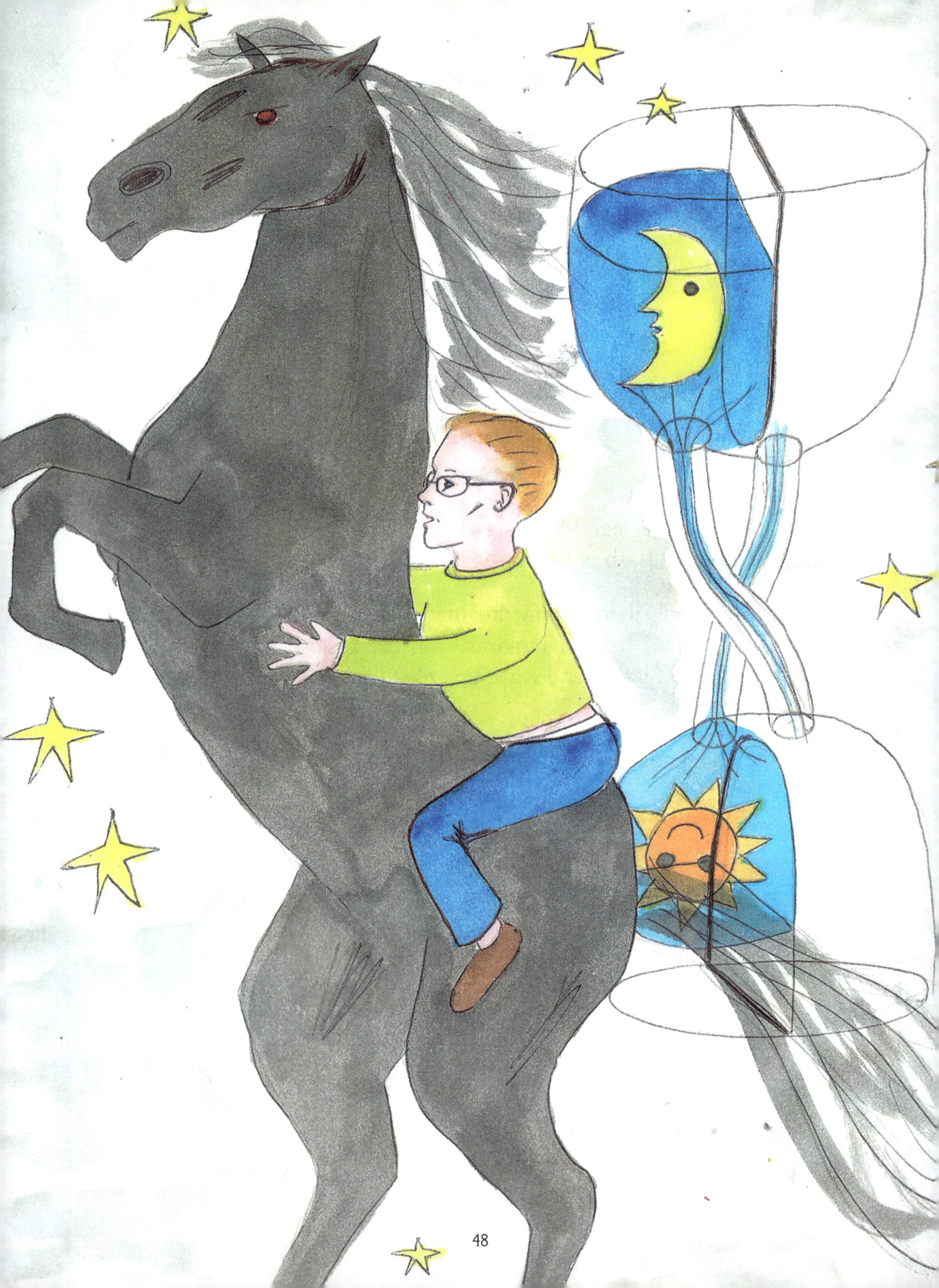

"I'm guessing you don't want to be a horse then?" Tyler asked.

Night Mare nodded forcefully, her black mane flying as she bucked.

"Let's go get some help then!" And in one easy motion Tyler grabbed hold of her thick black mane and swung himself onto Night Mare's back.

"Are you sure that you want to come with me?" Night Mare asked through a series of snorts. "I have no idea where I am going or what we could be facing."

"Heck, adventure is my middle name!" Tyler laughed boastfully. "Besides, you need me!" And he gripped her mane tighter and urged her on.

Sage smiled. She did need him.

Out into the blackness of night the two raced, house to house, city to city, country to country. The Universal Hour Glass turned end to end night to day, day to night. Night Mare and Tyler raced through the sands forward through time. Try as they might though, they couldn't seem to beat the slippery sands of time to catch up with Sandman. Instead they ended up almost full circle, back at Sage's house just moments after Sandman left.

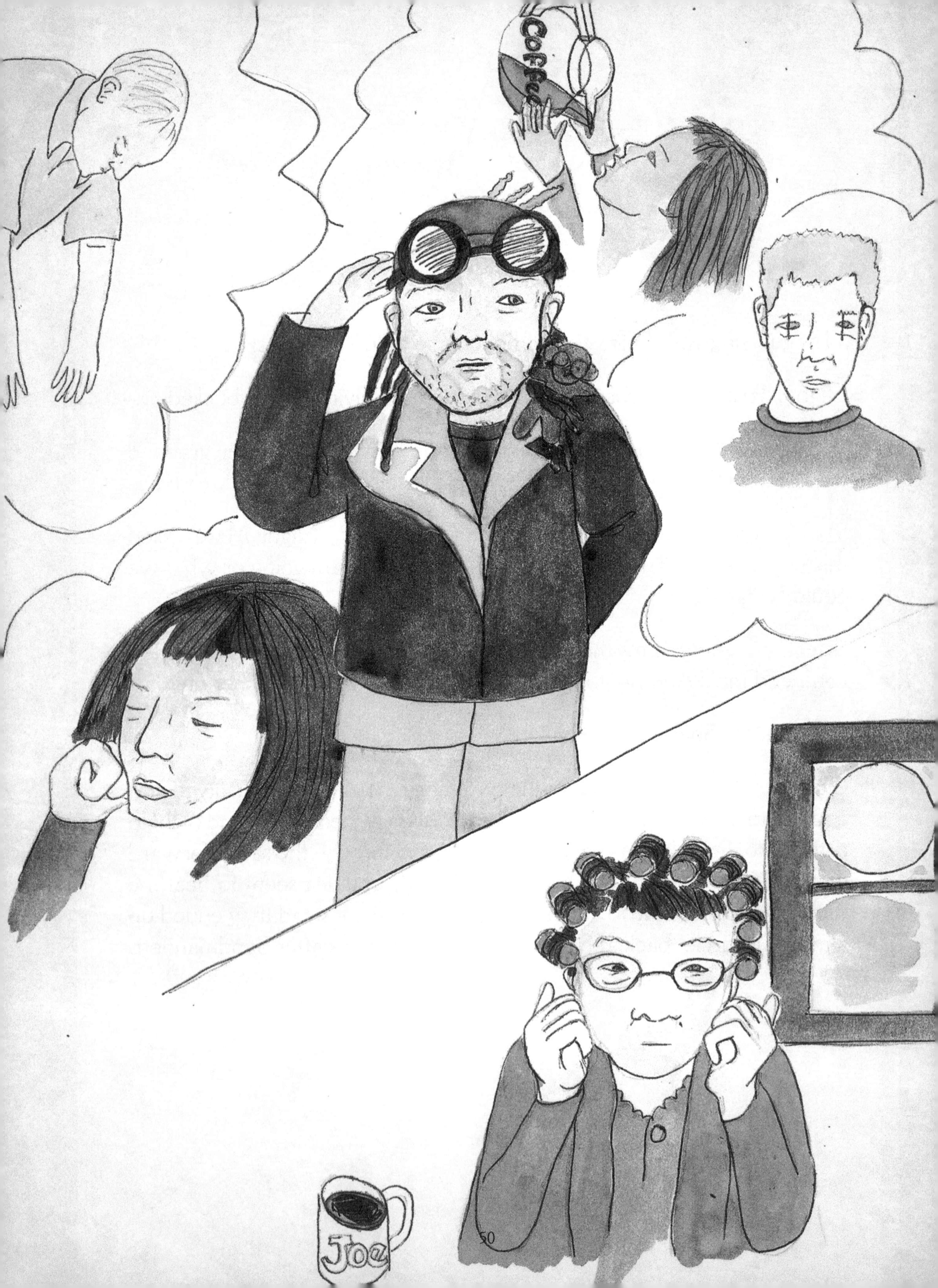
COFFEE
Joe

Having heard the whispers, Sandman knew of Night Mare's existence. He was under the impression though that she was the cause of all of the nightmares people were having. For, as Sandman went house to house on his regular nightly route around the globe, he found that people were now too afraid to sleep. As the world's population grew more tired, and grouchier, more people were refusing sleep. They were scared by their dreams. They no longer allowed Sandman into their homes to give them his gift. Instead, people downed pots of coffee and were constantly on their feet, jogging in circles. Some even used heavy-duty tape or tooth picks to keep their eyelids propped open. Everyone feared what the Sandman's sleep and Night Mare would bring.

Sandman needed to catch Night Mare. He was determined on this!

No longer sleeping either, Mother Mare feared her daughter might possibly never return to her normal form. Mother Mare waited up day and night to catch sight of Sage. She dearly missed her sweet, perky, mischievous, young daughter. Her daughter, now a black mare with fiery red eyes, would briefly visit her on the rounds. But the sight of her as a black mare broke her heart. Mother Mare was desperate to come up with a way to change Sage back. She just wished that Sandman would pay her a visit, and soon! He would know what to do!

52

Set to act, Mother Mare decided that she would grab hold of Night Mare's mane the next time she appeared. She was going to swing herself up on to her daughter's back and together they could conquer anything. When Night Mare appeared however, Mother Mare was startled to see Tyler already mounted upon her daughter.

Stunned, Mother Mare let go of her daughter's mane and stared up at the boy.

Night Mare whinnied, half-crazed, as the magic that had sent her on her nightly route began to pull her to leave. Mother Mare had to grab onto her again, quickly!

Tyler made a great effort to hold the bolting horse. "Grab on!" he yelled down at Mother Mare. "I can't hold her!" He reached out his hand as he felt the mare beneath him begin to buck. "Come on, take my hand!" he yelled to Mother Mare.

Quickly, Mother Mare reached out and grabbed Tyler's hand. With his help she managed to swing herself up behind him. And, in a flash Night Mare was gone. Through the night the three raced on, finding neither Blackie nor Sandman.

54

On and on they traveled and searched . . . .

They found a tour boat operator in Inverness, Scotland being chased by the Loch Ness Monster. Night Mare, Tyler, and Mother Mare worked together to ward off Nessie. The captain worked frantically to try and restart the boat engine to get himself and the tourists to safety.

In Shanghai, China kites at the kite festival were suddenly alive and attacking their line-handlers. Dragon kites circled and attacked, their open mouths shooting flames at the people on the ground. Night Mare, Tyler, and Mother Mare brandished scissors to cut the lines so that the winds would carry these monsters off into the upper atmosphere.

Back in the United States, the first game of the World Series was being played. Every batter had been allowed to walk the bases, as the balls being pitched were one-ton weights. The opposing team couldn't pick them up to throw. Tyler jumped down from Night Mare and took the pitcher's mound. Unaffected by the players dreams, Tyler picked up a ball and hurled it at the batter who struck it for a homerun. The crowds in the stands cheered wildly and Tyler took a bow.

56

Safely home again from their rounds, Mother Mare quickly piled a circle of rocks around Night Mare to keep her spirit from fleeing into the night on another route. The mare was exhausted and happy for the rest. Sandman however had left some sand as a trap to stop Night Mare's helpers. Try as they might, neither Mother Mare nor Tyler could keep their eyes open to keep watch. Tyler vanished back to his own house while Mother Mare slept on the couch.

Blackie appeared before Sandman though. He kicked away the circle of stones that magically restrained Night Mare, and both he and Sage were gone the next morning.

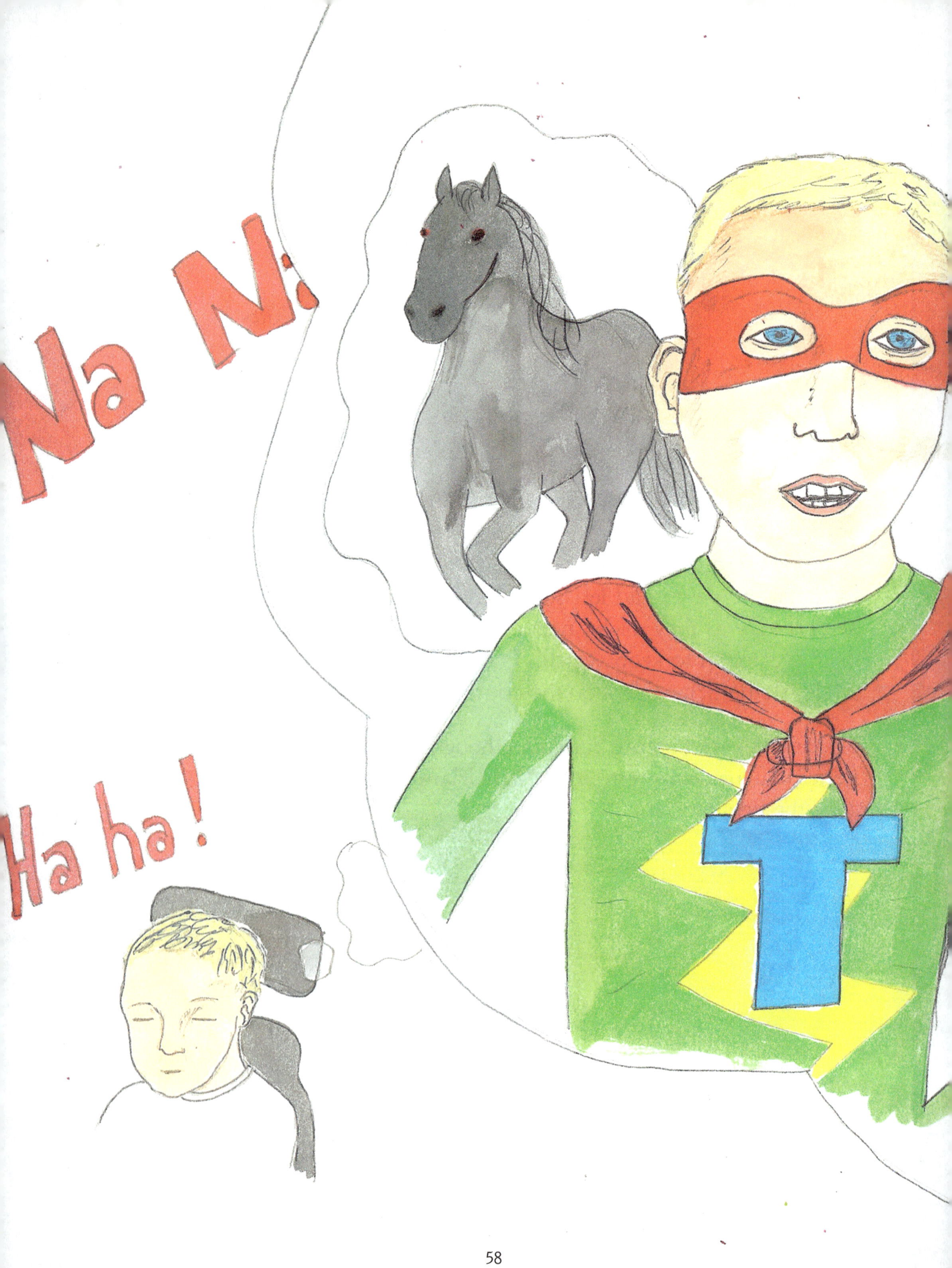
Na Na
Ha ha !

Sage was no longer at school days to protect the other kids from bullies. Peter and his gang were now even bullying Tyler. Tyler was glad when night returned and he had his dreams and his freedom. His need to free Night Mare, no, Sage, was now greater than ever.

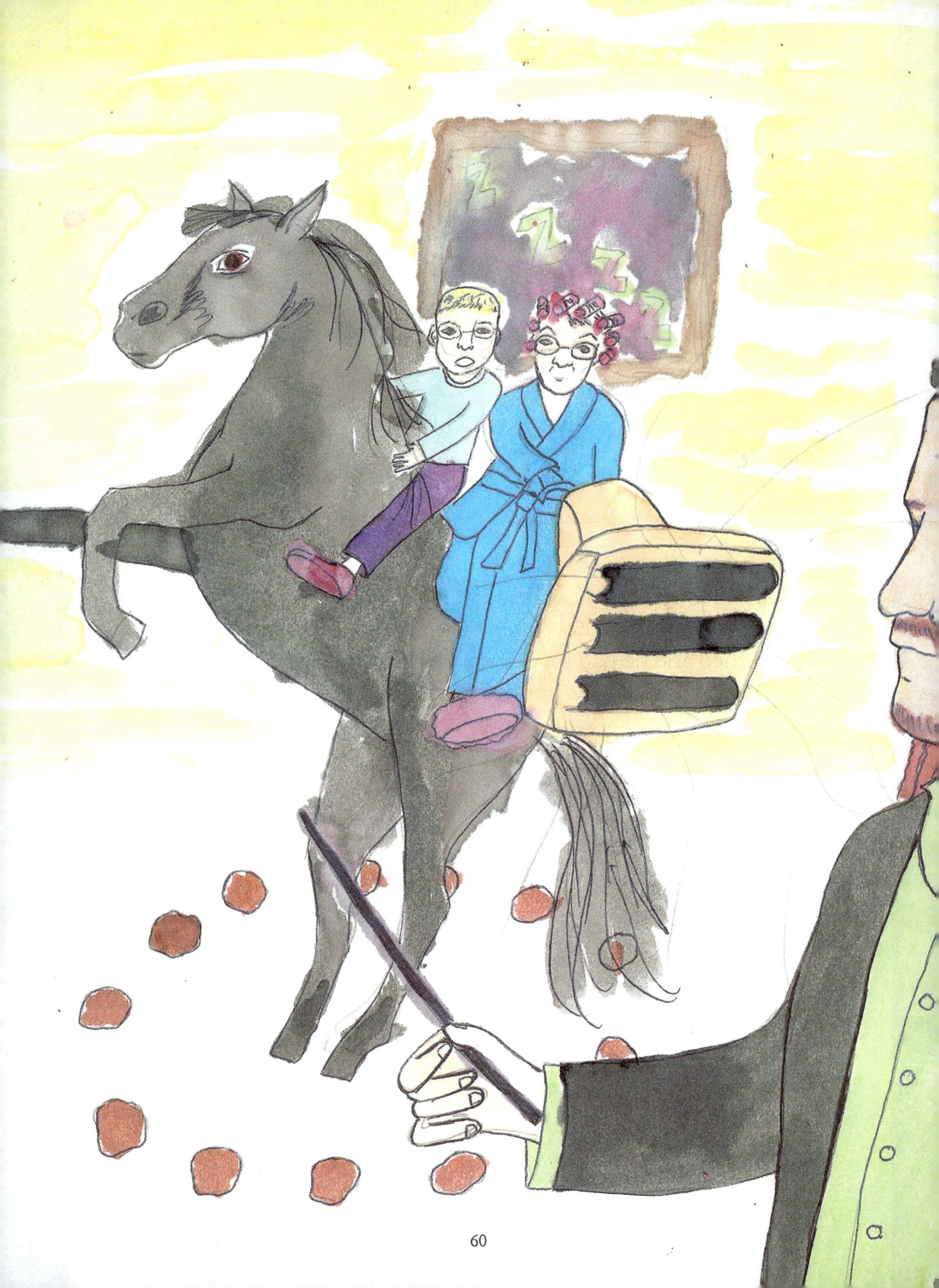

The next night Mother Mare and Tyler circled Night Mare with rocks again. This time Mother Mare was prepared and had a vacuum cleaner at the ready to suck up any sleeping sand that might be used to put them to sleep again. Mother Mare and Tyler waited, and waited, and waited . . . . Finally, Sandman came by on his rounds.

Sandman was startled to find Night Mare at the Mare house. He had sought her out for so long that he had almost given up hope of catching up to her.

Tyler elbowed the tired Mother Mare as she began to drift off to sleep.

Mother Mare lurched, her eyes fluttering open as she was suddenly awake. "You!" she shrieked angrily upon seeing Sandman. "You change my daughter back this instant!" she demanded.

"Hello Tyler. Good to see at least someone's enjoying their sleep!" Sandman nodded to the boy sitting astride Night Mare. He returned his glance to Mother Mare then. "I was thinking more along the lines of banishing her, my dear lady," he continued calmly, eyeing the weary woman. "You say this horse is your daughter though? How can this be?" He waved his wand at them both to come down off the frightened horse so that he could smite it.

Neither Tyler nor Mother Mare would budge. They were sure that Sandman wouldn't use his wand against Sage if they remained on her back.

Mother Mare then pressed forward to explain to Sandman about the sleeping sand incident at school and her daughter's transformation into Night Mare by his wayward intern.

Tyler could barely contain himself and his excitement now. "It was awesome! You should have been there to see all of our adventures!" he blurted. He stopped then, realizing he had said too much. Mother Mare was glaring at him.

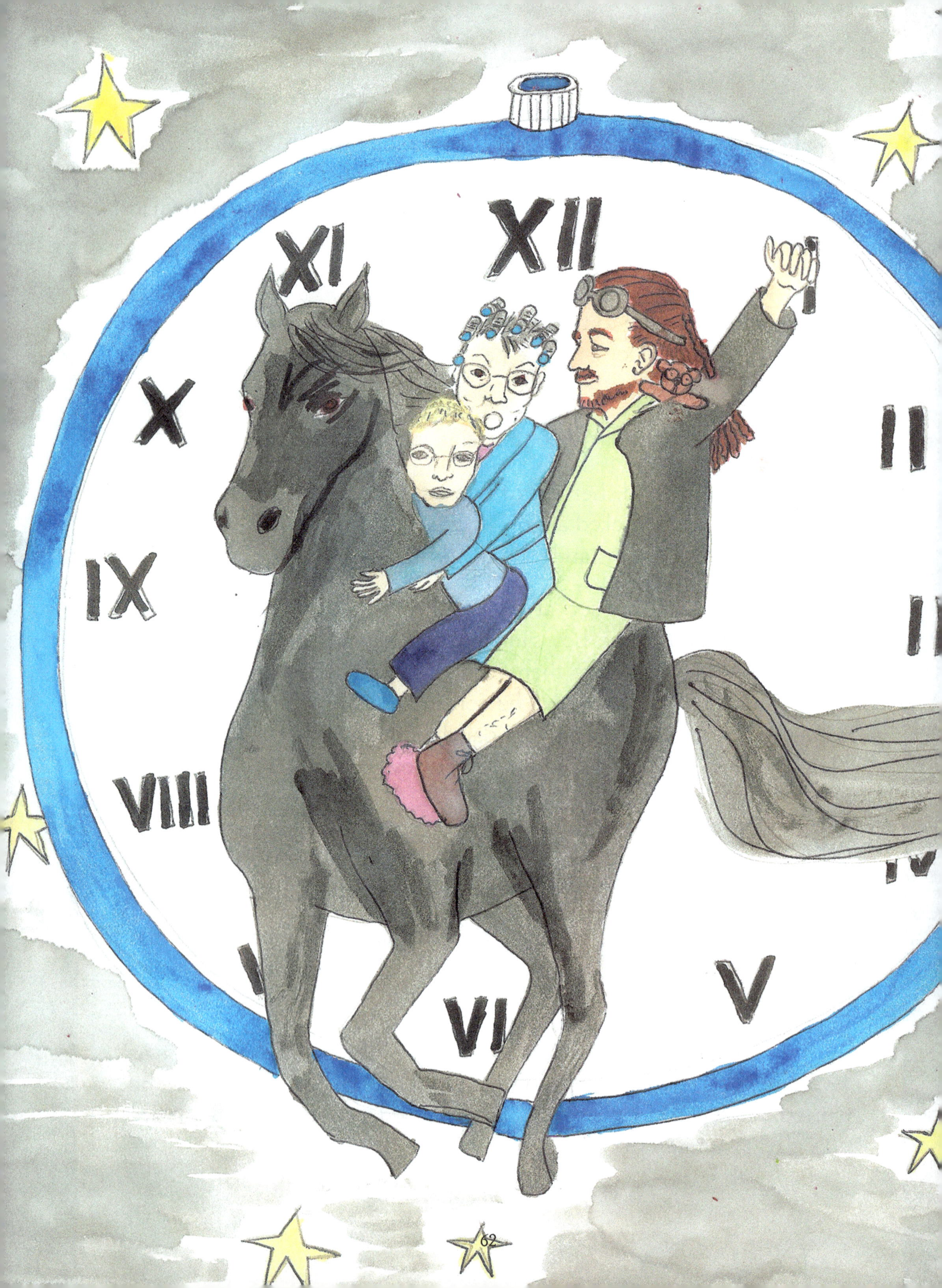
XII
XI
X
IX
VIII
VI
V
II

"This was caused by my intern Blackie?" Sandman questioned, outraged. Sandman now began to kick away the circle of stones. Grabbing a lock of Night Mare's mane he sprang onto her back behind Tyler and Mother Mare as she was being pulled away to follow her route. "Unfortunately Blackie's the only one who can reverse all of this I'm afraid . . . . We need to find him if your daughter is ever to be turned back into a little girl. We need to find him if I am ever to get some peace again in my work, and people in their lives." Sandman urged Night Mare on to race her route faster this night then she ever had.

64

The four-some galloped through homes, through dreams, through nightmares, and through the mists of time for what seemed an eternity. Finally, back at Rocky Forest they came upon the nightmare of the school's primary bully, Peter, as he slept in his room. He was dreaming about school and the desire to become the biggest, worst bully ever. Blackie was there too. In a puff of black sand, Peter was now having part of his wish come true. The black sands of nightmares though were not aiding Peter in this quest. Rather, they were burying him under the heaviness of his wish. He was now the victim as he found himself almost completely buried in black sand. Surrounded by his former victims, Peter raised a hand desperately for help, almost as if he could see Sandman and Night Mare and the others.

Tyler, the only one not affected by the effects of the black sands, and having a fresh and vivid imagination jumped into action. Quickly, he conjured Mother Mare's vacuum cleaner and sucked up all the black sand that buried the boy. Freed, Peter got up from the ground and raced around the corner of the school to hide from any further dreams.

Outraged, Blackie vanished in an instant.

Tyler raced back to his companions and re-mounted Night Mare. The four-some raced on to look for Blackie, catching up with him once again in Tyler's own bedroom.

66

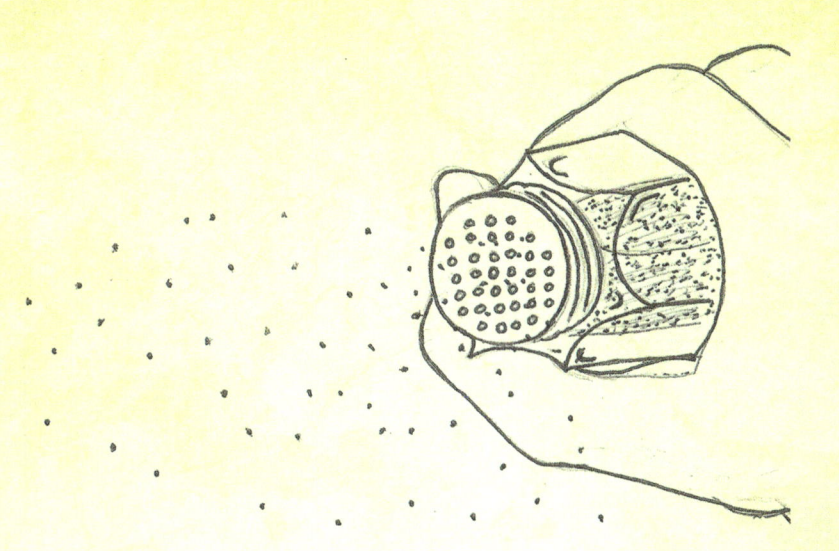

Frustrated by Tyler's refusal to live out the nightmares intended for all to share in, Blackie blew fistful after fistful of his black sand at the sleeping child. He was becoming increasingly agitated as the boy still wouldn't give in to the bad dreams. Blackie knew that if he couldn't turn everyone's dreams into nightmares he had no hope of ever ending Sandman's career. Tyler was now the last holdout in the non-magical realm.

"Come child, succumb! Fall unto these black sands and be mine at last!" came Blackie's shrieking troll chant.

It was a standoff between Blackie's black nightmare sands and Sandman's golden sands of restful sleep. Both magical creatures stood, fists-full of sand at the ready over Tyler's bed.

Tyler, Mother Mare, and Night Mare stood aside watching in dismay, desperate to find something that they could do to help to push the odds in Sandman's favor. They just couldn't let Tyler succumb to Blackie's plan!

An idea came to Tyler then. Spying his night care attendant snoozing over in the corner of his room, he looked to see if she had her usual midnight snack. He was overjoyed to see her usual hard boiled eggs and shaker full of pepper ready at the table. Racing over to the snack, Tyler leaned in and took a long whiff of the pepper. Then, just as the Sandman and Blackie simultaneously threw their sands at one another over the sleeping boy's form, in that briefest split of a second, the sleeping boy sneezed, blowing both batches of sand in Blackie's direction.

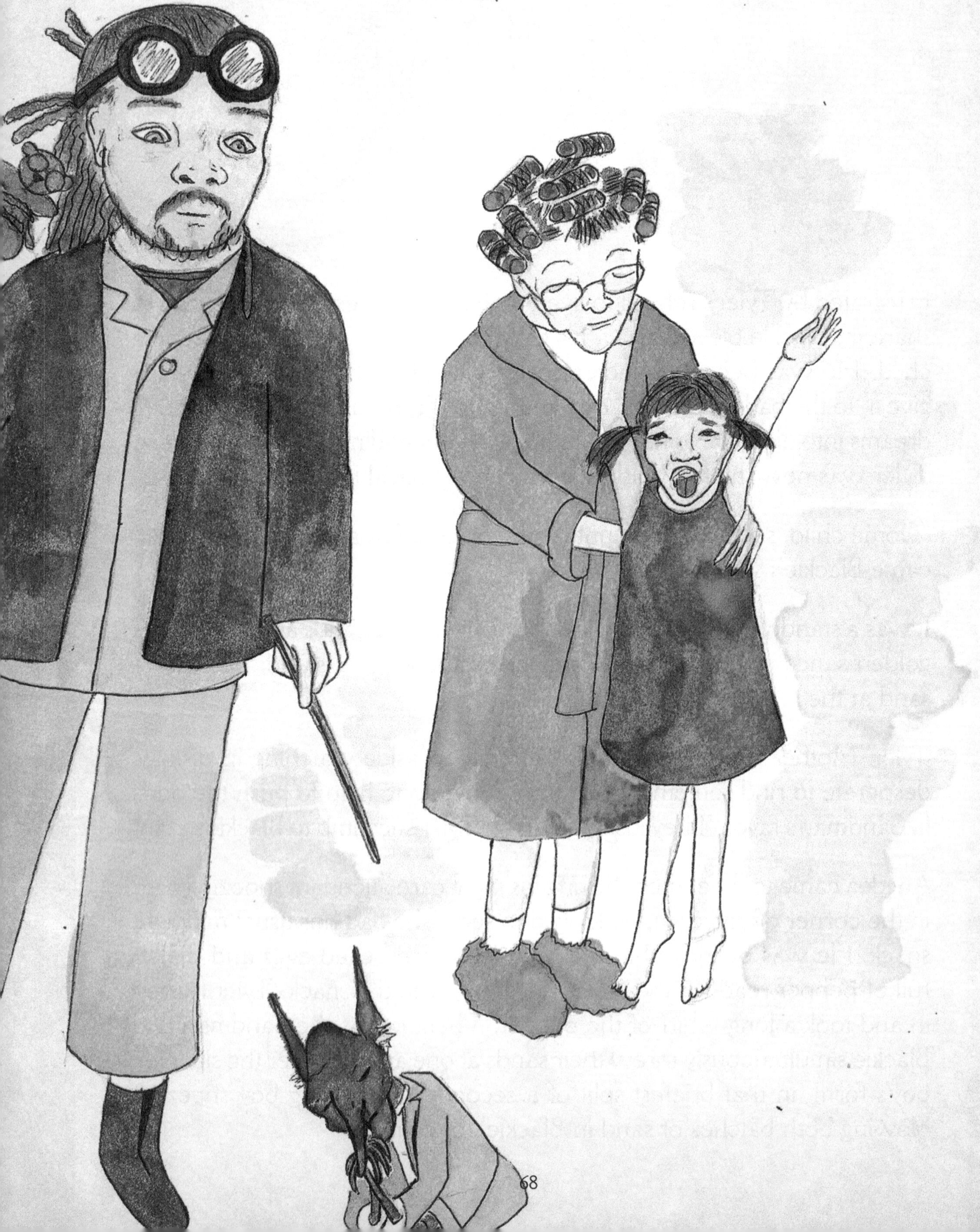

Blackie was out cold. Deep in sleep the ex-intern's dreams terrorized him. Blackie was again jobless in the magic realm with no prospects of a future. Spying Sandman, Blackie's dream-self quickly fell at his feet, begging Sandman to spare him from his nightmare.

"Release Sage from the form of Night Mare!" Tyler demanded of Blackie.

The dream-Blackie drew his magnetic wand from his pocket and the black sands were instantaneously withdrawn from the mare. Immediately, Night Mare was transformed back to her original self, a little girl . . . Sage.

Having little sympathy for his former intern, Sandman yanked Blackie's magnetic wand from his hands then and reluctantly released the troll from his own black sands that taunted him. He was careful however to leave his own golden sleep sands in effect.

It was over!

Sage and Mother Mare embraced. After many many long moments of crying and kisses, finally, reluctantly, Mother Mare released her daughter and went to Tyler's bed. Mother Mare looked fondly upon the boy as the hero that he was. She bent to kiss his forehead. "Thank you!" she whispered.

Tyler's dream-self had vanished. He was now sleeping in his own bed.

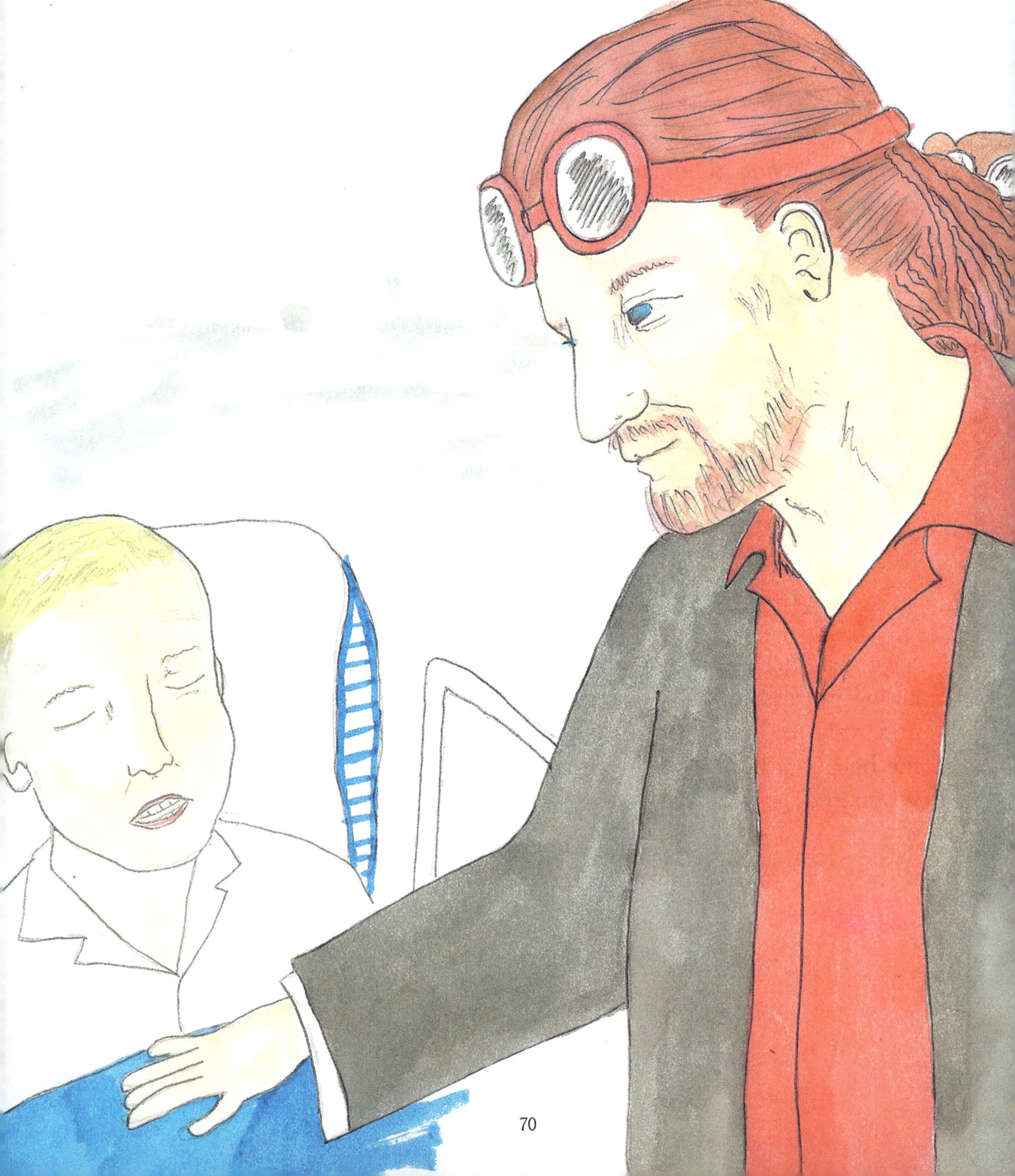

Impressed by Mother Mare's courage and steadfastness, Sandman offered her a hearty handshake and the vacated internship. She would be the first mortal he had ever hired. He knew though that she would be an excellent employee. Mother Mare readily accepted the offer.

Sandman then turned and went to Tyler. He leaned in to whisper into the sleeping child's ear. "Complete school. Afterwards, if you are interested, I would be honored to offer you a position as well. Your friendship and bravery have proved your abilities above all others!" He touched the boy's shoulder, offering him silent assurances, and Sandman, Mother Mare, and Sage vanished back to their own homes.

72

Sandman let Sage's punishment stand. After all, she had taken some of his golden sleeping sands to use for pranks in the first place. After a week at home doing as many chores as her mother could think up, Sage returned to school with renewed appreciation. Sage befriended the bullies (though she still had to put Peter in his place every so often), smiled more at Micah (who would now return her smile), and every day at recess she and her best friend, Tyler, were inseparable.

Racing his wheel chair around the playground, Sage recounted to all of their other friends the great adventures she and Tyler had shared. With Sandman's magic, and the supervision of Mother Mare, the two had many magical adventures in the realm of sleep and magic (though only on non-school nights).

Also by this author:

On the Way of the Half Kings

Ode to the Peanut Butter Sandwich

Coming soon:

Christmas Night Mare